World's End in Winter

Monica Dickens, the great-grand-daughter of Charles Dickens, lives with her husband and two children in America, surrounded by horses, cats and dogs. Author of the famous *One Pair of Hands* and *One Pair of Feet*, autobiographies of her early life, she has written such successful novels as *Kate and Emma* and is also the author of *Follyfoot* and *Dora at Follyfoot*, bestsellers published in Piccolo.

Also published in Piccolo are her other books in the World's End series: *The House at World's End, Summer at World's End* and *Spring Comes to World's End*.

Also by Monica Dickens in Piccolo

Monica Dickens
Cover illustration and text illustrations by Peter Charles

World's End in winter

A Piccolo Book
Pan Books in association with
William Heinemann Ltd

First published 1972 by William Heinemann Ltd
This edition published 1973 by Pan Books Ltd,
Cavaye Place, London SW10 9PG
in association with William Heinemann Ltd
2nd printing 1975
ISBN 0 330 23749 7
© Monica Dickens 1972

Printed in Great Britain by
Richard Clay (The Chaucer Press) Ltd, Bungay, Suffolk

The author and publishers are indebted to the Hon. Verona Kitson, Chairman of the Riding for the Disabled Association, for her help and advice.

The lines from *Right Royal* by John Masefield on page 102 are quoted by permission of the Society of Authors as the literary representative of the estate of John Masefield.

One

It was going to be a cold one.

Even before September was out, Oliver's skewbald pony coat had begun to grow as busily as if he were going to spend the winter on his native Welsh hills.

The swallows left the barn, and neither head, legs nor tail of the tortoise had been seen for two weeks. Brown and yellow leaves whirled before the wind, as hedges and trees closed the tips of their twigs over next spring's buds. Henry the ram was wool walking without legs. Leonora rolled a good insulation of mud into her grey donkey coat, and lay down if you tried to brush her. Charlie got a squint from trying to see through shaggy hair. He had to be trimmed with hedge clippers because Michael had dropped the scissors into the pond, trying to cut grass under water. The fish had disappeared to wherever fish go.

The chickens went to roost earlier every evening, and the cats and dogs spent more time in front of the stove. Soon it would be too dark to ride after school, so Carrie and Michael and their friend Lester took the horses out as much as they could before the bitter dark days closed down.

One clear afternoon which might almost have been spring, if it had not smelled of autumn, they cantered across the big stubble field where the wheat was cut, jumping the few straw bales that had been left. John and Peter took them in their stride. When these were two together, Oliver hopped on and off, changing legs on top as if he were taking a bank at the Dublin Horse Show.

At the far end of the field, they turned into the narrow, high-banked road that led into the village where a stream ran alongside the street. The cottages here were like castles,

7

with a moat outside the garden, and a bridge to cross to the front path.

On the outskirts of the village was the big red brick house that had stood empty long enough for people to say it was haunted. Its bridge was the end of a wide asphalt drive. The padlocked white gate had a sign saying Brookside, with a board nailed underneath, 'FOR SALE. KEEP OUT', like a 'Don't Touch' notice in a china shop.

'If I lived there,' Carrie said, 'I'd have a drawbridge across the stream, and pull it up when I saw certain people coming.'

'If you lived there, you'd be glad to see anybody,' Lester said. They had stopped their horses in the lane to look at the house beyond the weed-grown drive. It looked back at them with blank windows that no one had looked out of for two years.

'Is it really haunted?' Carrie whispered, as if the windows were listening as well as watching.

'Yes.' Lester knew everything that went on over a large area of this countryside. What he didn't know he invented, but it usually turned out to be true anyway.

'What by?'

'Voices. Sighs. Phantom hounds. A baby crying. Miss Etty told me.' Miss Etty was the lady who had built a brand new bungalow round a tree rather than cut it down. It grew diagonally through a corner of her sitting room, and her birds sat in it. 'Want to go round and see what we can hear?'

Michael said, 'No,' but the others had turned back, following the stream for a place to cross, so he pulled his pony's head up from the grass and went with them.

John and Peter jumped the narrow stream quite easily. Oliver slithered halfway down the bank, trampled his feet like a cat, leaped straight up into the air, landed with all four feet together and scrambled up the opposite bank. Michael picked himself up from the edge of the stream and climbed after him.

'You should hang on to the mane,' Carrie said in her

Riding Instructor voice, which annoyed Michael, and usually made Em get off whichever horse she was riding and go indoors.

'I did.' Michael held up a muddy handful of Oliver's mane.

They rode round the tall hedge that surrounded Brookside's garden, and got in through a gate at the back with a broken latch. There was a tennis court, a small neglected swimming pool, a round thatched summer house like a beehive, and a stone terrace with french windows into the drawing room. They tied their horses to the wire fence round the tennis court and stood with their ears pressed against the long windows, to see what they could hear.

When you press your ear to a window pane, you can hear the sea wind in it, like a conch shell, and the whisper and creak of your own hair growing.

No ghosts. No wails or sighs. The house held its breath to see what they would do.

The long drawing-room was empty of furniture, with a bare floor and the top halves of two brooding ladies holding up the mantelpiece on either side of the brass grate. They were brooding about the weight of the mantelpiece, which had flattened the tops of their heads, like the back of a baby's head if nobody ever turns it in its cot.

Staring at their blind marble eyes, Michael leaned hard against the window. A pane of glass cracked like a rifle shot, and tinkled into the silence of their held breath.

Lester put his hand carefully through the jagged glass and turned the lock and they went in.

They went all over the house, listening. It was a prosperous but dull kind of house. Rooms and cupboards and staircases in predictable places. Flowered wallpaper upstairs. Modern tiled kitchen and bathroom. Prosperous but dull people had lived tidily here. Not restless haunters. No voices murmured of old tragedies on the stairs. On the upper landing under the attic trap door, there was not even the whisper of mouse feet. In the round turret room at the corner, there was no hint of lavender where a betrayed girl had once fluttered her handkerchief. Not even her sigh.

Michael stopped holding on to Carrie's sleeve, and his eyes went back to their normal size under his ragged fringe. They were turning to go, when Lester suddenly stopped in the middle of the bare boards of the turret room. Outside, a wind was getting up. It rattled the long leaves of the laurel shrubbery, breathed deeply through the garden firs, and ran along the gutter like a flute. Dogs barked, chasing something. Overhead, a jet plane churned, high up. There was no other sound, but Lester stood with his pointed ears pricked, eyes wide, mouth open, nose flared, fingers feeling the air, listening with all his senses.

'Hear it?'

An army of ants crept up Carrie's spine. She shook her head.

'*Listen.*'

There it was – a faint, thin wailing.

A banished spirit trying to get in?

A nun bricked up in the walls?

'The baby,' Lester whispered. 'The baby that cries.'

Michael pressed against Carrie and stuffed both hands into his mouth to keep from shrieking.

Then they heard the voices. Lester stood at the side of the window and glanced down like a sniper. The tall shrubbery hid the gate and the front drive. The wailing again, and then in a pause of the wind, a man's voice.

'Damn thing's stuck.'

Someone was trying to get into the house.

Moving as one, Carrie, Lester and Michael fled out of the room and down the passage. At a window over the front door, they slowed just long enough to look down. A man in a check cap was fighting with the lock. Behind him, a well-dressed woman and a tall man carrying a child with thin legs dangling in red tights. He had turned back to say something to the woman, and the child's pale face, flopped sideways on his shoulder, was turned up to the window with dark, uncaring eyes that looked, but did not seem to see.

They ran down the stairs and out through the broken

10

french door, untied the horses and got away through the back gate. They jumped the stream farther down where a banked corner hid them from the house – no trouble with Oliver jumping towards home – three strides across the road and into the stubble field, spreading out to gallop each their own line, hair and manes and tails streaming with the wind.

'Did that child see us?' Carrie bent to wipe her wet eyes and nose on John's mane as they waited at the end of the field for Michael to catch up.

'Who knows?' Lester rode bareback with a halter, loose and easy, riding all wrong, but riding Peter just right. 'She looked drugged.'

'Kidnapped? She was too big to be carried.'

'Or to cry like a baby. *If that was her crying.*'

The ants again, crawling up the back of Carrie's neck into her wind-lifted hair.

'She looked not there.' Michael came up, and turned Oliver's head into the wind to help him get back his breath, although he was panting more than the pony. 'Do you think she was dead?'

By the time they had trotted through the wood and along the edge of the beanfield and round the flank of the darkening hill into their own lane, they could almost wonder if they had imagined her.

Mr Mismo was out in his barnyard, lagging a standpipe with straw and sacking and baling twine.

They stopped to tell him that they had seen the house agent showing Brookside to someone. A house changing hands was quite an event in this quiet countryside where nothing much happened except birth and death and marriage, and not much of those.

'I wonder if they'll buy it.' Carrie shivered and turned her polo neck up round her chin. With the sun gone down, there was no exhilaration in the wind.

'Not a chance.' Mr Mismo stood with his stumpy legs apart in boots as wide as sewer pipes, his arms behind his back to appraise the horses like a sergeant-major inspecting a drill squad. 'No money about these days.' Having settled the fate of Brookside, he said sharply, 'Them horses been lathering up. You ride 'em too hard.'

'It's good for them to sweat.' Carrie put on her instructive voice. 'It gets rid of the poisons of the system, you see, and regulates the temperature, so that—'

'They'll founder.' Mr Mismo always saw disaster. 'Get them on home out of this perishing wind, or you'll have a stableful of coughs before the winter's half begun. It's going to be a cold one.'

Two

Carrie's younger sister Em, and Liza who had lived with them like an older sister since she left her unhappy home for good, went to the Church Jumble Sale to buy jerseys and scarves.

Liza was a violent character with long smouldering red hair and extreme loves and hates. She sang strange rude songs that she had learned from the other lawless girls at Mount Pleasant, which was a place nearby where they sent girls who were too bad to go to school and too young to go to prison. She swore and threw things and would clout you and hug you all in the same movement, and make you laugh and cry at once.

Em was the most domesticated of the family, more of a house person, like a cat, which was what she thought she had been in a former life. She and Liza did the cooking at World's End. Sometimes it was marvellous. Sometimes even the dogs were doubtful. They also did the shopping, when there was any money in the blue and white striped sugar jar. Sugar was in the jar that said 'Tea', and Tea was in 'Rice'.

As the weather got colder, they went round the house stuffing newspaper into window gaps, and then they went to the Church Jumble Sale and bought some jerseys and scarves and rubber boots and a white woollen hood for Michael.

It framed his cheerful face and sticky chin like a Crusader's chain mail. He wore it constantly, sometimes in bed. It was the best thing that had happened to him so far this winter.

The first morning when he wore the hood to school, a crude boy called Gregory Ferris fell on him with hoots and yells.

'E's wearing my old 'ood! 'Ere look, Walter, look at poor old Mike, got to wear me old clothes. My mum wasn't even going to give it to the Jumble, because she didn't think it would fetch nothing.'

Michael stood with his fists clenched, his cheeks red from rage and from the chilly ride behind John in the dogcart, with the hood cuddling his ears.

'Didn't ought to be allowed, did it?' Gregory's toady friend tutted and pursed his mouth, like women gossiping in the village. 'All those poor children living on their own in that ruin. Not right, is it?'

He was quoting his mother. Most of the local children envied the Fieldings living with their animals at World's End, with no one more grown up than their brother Tom, and Liza who was often more childish than anyone.

After the last spot of trouble with Mrs Loomis, the headmistress, Tom had made Michael promise not to fight any more, so he stuck out his tongue far enough to lick the drop off his nose and turned to go into school.

But behind him, the crude voice of Gregory Ferris sneered, 'You're right, it's not right. Where's his dad then, that's what they say.'

'I told you.' Michael swung round. 'He's sailing round the world with my mother.'

'Ha bloody ha,' jeered Gregory, and Michael was into the fight with arms and legs and head, the two of them

13

scrabbling on the gritty cement playground, Walter hopping round like a referee.

Michael was winning. He usually won fights. That was why he started them. But as Gregory scrambled up to run away – creeps like him never fought to a finish – he grabbed at Michael's hood and it turned right round on his

Gregory pulled Michael's hood over his head, and as he did so Michael hit out at the pane of glass.

head and muffled him. He hit out blindly, not at Gregory, but at the glass pane of the school door.

It did not shatter, because it was reinforced with wire, but it broke right across with the same rifle crack as the window at Brookside (two broken windows was sure to mean a third).

'That will cost you two pounds, little boy.' Mrs Loomis, who never could remember names, even of people like

Michael who were constantly on the carpet of her office, lifted the hood off his head and dangled it like a tea cosy. The small soft moustache along her upper lip stood out like cat's fur when it was cold.

Michael snatched his white hood from her and ran out across the playground.

He did not go into school. He spent the morning sitting in the hollow of John's brown back in the shed where the baker let Carrie keep the horse while his van was on the bread rounds.

'What are you doing, Mike?' At dinnertime, Carrie came out with carrots for John from the school cook.

'I owe Mrs Bloomers two pounds.'

Carrie understood why he was with John, brooding in his hood. He might as well have said twenty pounds.

Tom had a job at the zoo hospital, where many of the animals were wintered when the zoo was closed. Liza was working for Alec Harvey the vet, who was as poor as they were, since he was always treating animals free for people who were even poorer.

He kept promising Liza a rise. 'That'll be the day,' she told him, on hands and knees sweeping up the rack of expensive test tubes she had just broken.

Carrie and John earned a bit of money taking horse manure round to the gardeners of the housing estates at Newtown, but all the gardeners were indoors these days with their shoes off, watching television. She helped Mr Mismo with his pigs and cows, and Mrs Mismo, who thought food was more important than money (which it was), paid her in sausage rolls and big currant biscuits called Fat Rascals.

Em, using her business name of Esmeralda, did baby-sitting for local mothers. If they were decent children, she was decent to them. If they were vile, she was vile back. Mrs Potter gave her a bonus if little Jocelyn, who bit, actually drew blood.

Michael sold inventions where he could. Fireplace trivets

15

and flowerpot holders made from horseshoes. Stools made out of broomsticks and upside-down cake tins. Potato mashers made of wire coathangers. Floor polishers made of bricks covered with felt. You tied them round your feet and skated. He also did shopping errands for a crippled old lady called Miss Cordelia Chattaway, and she gave him ten pence every Sunday for wheeling her to church and finding the hymns.

Everyone helped to make money, but there was never more than just enough to feed all the two-legged and four-legged mouths.

'Dogs can eat table scraps,' Aunt Valentina had said when Em asked for a case of dog food for her birthday. But at World's End, there never were any scraps.

'A horse can keep fat on good old Doctor Green,' Mr Mismo said. But John and Peter and Oliver worked hard and needed oats as well as grass. Soon there would be no goodness in the winter grazing, and there would be hay to buy.

The roof needed patching where autumn gales had blown some corner tiles off. The rainwater pump needed a new valve. Everyone needed new shoes except the horses, since the blacksmith was more important than the shoe shop, and the old black cooking stove was cracked right across and would be lucky if it hung on till spring.

'Money doesn't matter,' Mother always said. And that was true. As long as you had some.

'When my book is published,' their father had said, 'we shall all be rich and famous.' The book was *Sailor of the Seven Seas*, with photographs of Mother in the rigging. He had not written it yet.

Meanwhile, there was two pounds to pay Mrs Loomis for the broken glass. And if those people with the strange pale child did buy Brookside and guessed from the hoof-marks who might have broken the drawing-room window, would that be two pounds too?

On the evening of Michael's fight with Gregory Ferris, Tom came home from the zoo tired and cross. A ferret had

16

died of pneumonia. Jan Lynch, Tom's boss, had said in her clipped voice that did not show if she was annoyed, angry or furious, 'Might have lived if you'd kept its front end propped.'

'How can you keep a blasted ferret propped up?' Tom raged, slumped at the kitchen table, legs stuck out on Charlie's shaggy back, tearing great chunks off the crust of a new loaf. 'How can I do *everything*? It's always my fault. I'm fed up. I'm going to tell that woman... Yesterday she told me to get my hair cut. I ask you. Just because it got singed in a bunsen burner in the lab.' He dragged his long, knuckly hand through his flopping hair, leaving crumbs in it. 'I'm fed up. Life's too short ...' etc, etc. When Tom was tired and cross, he smouldered with frustrated fires, flinging his long arms and legs and hair about, kicking furniture. The cats went up to a safer level of counter and shelves and watched. A runty marmoset he had brought home from work stuck its round eyes and tufted ears out of the front of his shirt to see what was going on.

'I'll leave. I'll go to college and come out a better vet than Jan is. Then she'll be sorry.'

'Surprised, more like.' Liza giggled.

Tearing at the loaf, Tom shouted at her to shut up and leave him alone. Charlie got up and went to lie somewhere else. The marmoset blinked and drew its head back inside Tom's shirt. Caesar the five-toed tortoiseshell cat jumped off the table and made a dignified exit through the hole in the back door, which had a swinging rubber flap made from the mudguard of a lorry.

Carrie took a snaffle bit and a pair of stirrups out of the saucepan where they had been soaking and went off to polish them in another room.

Even Liza, who did not care what she said to anyone, did not shout back at Tom to shut up himself and stop mutilating the bread. She whispered to Michael, 'Don't tell him about the window now.'

Echoes of Mother. *'Don't tell your father till he's had his dinner.'*

Even Tom and Liza, even at their age, were already catching the grown-up disease of when to tell what.

When a thing had to be said, it had to be said.

Michael said it, but with his back turned to Tom, looking out of the window and fiddling with a thread in the curtain, toes turned in so far that one shoe was over the other, a draughty gap of skin between his shrunk jersey and sagging trousers, woollen hood jammed down tight over his ears so that he could not hear Tom being angry.

After a while, when he had frayed the curtain enough to poke a finger through, he turned and saw that Tom was not being angry. Tom was not being anything. Tom was not even in the room. Nor was Liza. Nor were any of the dogs. Only Michael's mother was suddenly standing in the doorway with her arms held out.

'Have you got two pounds?' Michael asked her.

'Of course not.' Mother laughed. She hugged him. Nothing mattered.

Three

Their father had come home to start his book, *Sailor of the Seven Seas*, although he had not even completely sailed the first sea yet.

Six times he and Mother had set bravely forth in the *Lady Alice*. Six times they had been forced back by freak storms, a split spinnaker, leaking water tanks, a seized-up dynamo...

The first time they left to sail round the world, the *Daily Amazer*, which was going to print the story, had sent down a reporter and a photographer. The local band played 'Hearts of Oak', and the mayor came out on the quay with his chain clinking in the breeze to wish them 'Godspeed'.

The second time, the *Lady Alice* was cheered away by two boy scouts with trumpets, playing 'For Those in Peril on the Sea'.

The last time, there was no one at all, except a fisherman who cast the stern line off the bollard, and the town drunk who owed Dad some money and wanted to be sure he got away.

That was the voyage on which the generator seized up and the torch batteries fell overboard and the matches were pooped by a soaking stern wave. They sailed blind through a starless night and ended up on a millionaire's private beach in the Cape Verde Islands. The millionaire's gunmen had shot away half the storm jib before Dad could shout.

'Too late to start out again till next spring, so what I'm going to do' – in the lamplight, the gold ring in Dad's ear glittered against his curly black beard, his eyes glittered with the excitement of a new scheme – 'is hole up here and start the book and we'll soon be rich and famous.'

'So can I have two pounds?' Tom and Carrie and Em had forgotten tiresome daily details in the drama of the sea story, but Michael hung on to things like a puppy with a laundry line.

'Right away.' Dad tipped his chair on to its back legs to fish in the pocket of his faded, sea-shrunk trousers.

'Jerry—' Mother put out her thin brown hand, but he pulled out some coins and poured them from a height into Michael's cupped palms as if they were doubloons.

'How much is that?' Michael could not count any better than he could spell.

'Two pounds and nine pence,' Em said.

'Keep the change, my good man.' Dad closed Michael's fingers round the money.

'Jerry—' Mother said again, and he pulled his pocket inside out to show her that there was nothing left in it but a fishing float and a stub of pencil and a piece of caulking compound.

The next morning, which was a Saturday, with everybody

home but Tom and Liza, he was in great energy, demanding four fried eggs for brain fuel, sending everyone off in different directions to equip him for his new career.

Mother had to hunt up his old plaid dressing gown because authors always wore old plaid dressing gowns. Michael rode Oliver to the village for paper and pencils, and supplied wood for the sitting-room fire by his patent method of rolling logs through the window and down a board into the rusted washtub which was the wood box.

Carrie swept the room and pushed the litter off the table on to the floor.

Em looked for cushions to cover the holes in the cane chair. All the cushions had cats on them, so she brought down two thick books from the trunk that had been left in the attic long ago by the family who once lived here. The musty mysterious smell of the pages was more fascinating than what was printed on them. Em read like eating and was always hard up for a book, but you had to be pretty desperate to get through either *Glimpses of Old Lapland* or *Tabby Tinker's Teatime Tales for the Littlest Folk*.

In his dressing gown and frayed rope shoes, his pipe between his teeth to make him look bookish, Dad said goodbye to his family as if he were going to prison for a month and went into the front room and shut the door. It swung open. Every door in this slightly crooked house either creaked open when you shut it, or shut when you wanted it open.

'Shut that perishing door!'

No one did, since no one had opened it, so he banged it and kicked a footstool against it.

He opened it three times in the first half-hour, demanding tea, Michael to ride back to the village for pipe tobacco, Em and Mother to stop talking about childbirth on the stairs.

Mother always had her best conversations in odd places: kneeling in a cupboard looking for a sandal, halfway up a ladder, on the roof cleaning leaves out of the gutter. One of the best talks she and Em had ever had, about what dying was, had been in the far corner of a room into which they had trapped themselves by starting to paint the floor from the doorway.

At last the door banged shut, the footstool scraped on the tiles, and they heard no more. Mother and Em, who were cleaning the house, went up and down stairs with their shoes off. Carrie moved Leonora off the front lawn in case she brayed. The red hen Rubella, who might boast for half an hour after she laid an egg, was taken down cackling from her perch by Michael and held in front of a white-washed wall to hypnotize her into silence.

At lunchtime, Em went round to the front of the house and peered through the bare tangled branches of the jasmine to see how the book was going.

Her father had put two big logs on the fire and was sitting on the last bone of his spine in the sagging armchair, with his bottom almost on the floor and his feet on the fireplace bricks, reading *Tabby Tinker's Teatime Tales for the Littlest Folk*.

'How's he getting on?' Her mother was making Alice's All-purpose Soup with anything she could find – chicken wings, three stewed plums, half a corned beef sandwich, a cup of tea, a wilted lettuce – stewed up in a pot with barley.

'Working away like mad,' Em said.

'You'd better take his lunch in there.'

Em took a bowl of soup and some bread and cheese and knocked on the sitting room door.

'Go away, I'm busy.'

'I brought your lunch.'

'Thank God.' She heard his feet scrape down from the fireplace. 'Come in,' he grunted. 'Push the door hard.'

She pushed it open and stepped in over the footstool with the baking sheet she was using for a tray. He was sitting at the table, pencil going swiftly over the paper, the other hand raking through the thick curly hair that made Em forget to fuss with flattening her own curls when he was at home.

'How's it going?' She put down the baking sheet at the

other end of the table. She had put one of the last chrysanthemums in an eggcup of water, like the man in the film *Ladykiller*, who had brought his wife one perfect rose on her breakfast tray and then stabbed her with the butter knife.

'Marvellous.' He leaned his arm on the paper so that she could not see, and pulled the soup towards him with the other hand. 'Smells good. You make it, Emmy?'

'Yes.' Em had the habit of telling lies for not much reason. She was trying to cure herself of pointless ones, so that people would believe the ones that mattered.

'Stick to cooking. Never try this lark.'

A kitten that had sneaked in with Em was playing football with the crumpled papers on the floor. Em picked up the kitten and some of the papers with it. After lunch, she went into the hayloft over the barn and smoothed out the papers, which had only a few scrawled words on one side, and began to write a play.

Four

Lester came in the afternoon.

Carrie had gone up to the meadow to catch John. He usually came when she whistled, but today he stood staring at nothing with his ears lopped sideways, as if he were blind and deaf, and made her come to him.

From the wood, a squirrel chittered. It wasn't a squirrel. It was Lester. He climbed over the brass bedstead which mended one of the gaps in the hedge.

'Look what I found.'

It was a perfect round pink stone, like a wren's egg. He unscrewed the knob of the bedstead, put the egg into the hollow place and screwed it up again. He was storing things here for posterity. Thousands of years hence, a traveller from the planet Uranus would unscrew the knob with the strange instruments which were his hands, and marvel at these treasures which spoke to him through the centuries. The stone egg, an old farthing, a gold filling from Lester's mother's tooth, a dog's dew claw, a piece of Liza's red hair tied with cooked spaghetti gone hard again, and a twist of paper with a two-line poem by Carrie:

When the last car on earth has crashed and the last plane has fallen from the skies and the last rocket satellite has run its course,
There will still be the galloping wonder of beauty. There will still be a horse.

They walked up the hill to where John was dreaming. Lester said quietly, 'Peter', and instantly the lovely chestnut head with the white star that was shaped like an onion or like the dome of the Taj Mahal, according to how you saw it, swung up from behind the blackberry bushes.

They walked down the hill with a hand on their horses' necks.

'My mother and father are home,' Carrie said.

'I know.'

'How?'

'I heard his old car.'

'He's writing a book.'

'I know.'

'How?'

'Bessie Munce at the shop told me there'd been an emergency call for paper.'

As they came down to the gate, Lester said casually, 'Someone else has come too. The moving van is at Brookside. Those people.'

They looked at each other without needing to raise an eyebrow, or smile, or say, 'Let's ride over there.' Their eyes met and the plan was made.

Michael was in the stable putting the saddle on Oliver. In

23

the summer, the small Welsh pony was neat and glossy, with elegant legs and delicate seahorse head. Half-way into his winter shag, he was already taking on his giant panda look, legs stumpy, mane sticking out on both sides because his neck was too thickly furred for it to lie down.

'Those people are moving into Brookside.' Carrie looked over the half door. 'We're going to ride over there and you can confess about the window.'

'Why?'

'It will give us an excuse to investigate.'

'Not me.' Michael led Oliver out and got on quickly to ride off somewhere else. Oliver had let go his breath. The saddle slipped round under his stomach and Michael stepped off into a squawk of chickens. Oliver put down his head, trod on his rein, jerked up his head and broke the buckle end of the rein.

By the time Michael had been back to the house for a skewer and string to mend the rein, the others were ready, so he had to ride off with them, because Oliver would not go in a different direction from John and Peter.

The moving van in the drive of Brookside was too wide to get past, so they drew twigs and Carrie lost, and stayed with the horses while the others walked up to the house. Furniture and rolled carpets were going in. They walked behind an oversized sofa into the hall and through into the room where Michael had broken the window. The glass had been mended.

A man and a woman were standing at the end of the room by the flat-skulled ladies who held up the mantelpiece arguing where the sofa should go. The moving men set it down, picked it up again, went sideways with it like a crab with a heavy shell, set it down where the man pointed, dusted off their hands, and then had to bend and lift it and sidle off again to where the woman was standing.

'It was better over here.' He was a big ruddy man, losing his hair and waist and the veins in his nose.

'Nonsense, Brian.' The woman was tall and athletic, with squared-off shoulders and shining teeth and eyes, crackling

24

with health and energy. 'Come on, boys, let's try it sideways to the fireplace.'

She grinned, thinking the men liked her, but behind her back, they made terrible faces at each other as they picked up the awkward sofa.

When it was down, she turned coolly to Lester and Michael, as if she had seen them in the doorway all along and meant to make them wait.

'Is it the newspapers?' she asked in her voice for talking to tradespeople, high and clear, as if they must be deaf or stupid. 'Or groceries? Do you deliver?'

'Yes, Madam.' Lester picked up a piece of packing straw and stuck it behind his ear like a pencil.

'It's the window.' Michael frowned under his white hood. 'They've been cleaned thank you.'

'But you see, I—' As Michael moved to the french door, he saw that a small wheelchair stood on the terrace in a patch of late sun. In the chair, bundled in scarves and mittens and fur boots, was the child with the blank dark eyes.

She looked at him, but would not smile. He tapped on the glass and waggled his fingers in an experimental wave.

'Don't tease Priscilla, there's a good boy,' the woman said.

'She's cold.' Michael turned round.

'Nonsense. Spot of fresh air never hurt anybody. Now run along, kids. We're very busy here.'

'I broke your window.' Michael clenched his fists by his waist, elbows out, defensively.

'Oh well, never mind.' She tossed aside his confession breezily. 'Off you go.'

Michael held his ground. 'What's wrong with your little girl?' He gave her his honest, innocent stare, which usually got results.

'She had an accident.'

'Can't she smile?'

'She can smile when she wants to.'

'Can't she walk then?'

Stepping between Michael and the window, the father said, 'It's just that Priscilla isn't as strong as our other children.' And added unnecessarily, 'They're *both* in their school teams for *everything*.'

He pushed Michael towards the door. 'What's wrong with your leg?'

'Nothing,' Lester answered for him.

'Then why's he limping?'

'It's shorter than the other.'

'Can't it be seen to?' the woman asked, as if Michael was a torn blind or a dripping tap.

'Not without cutting a bit off the other one,' Lester ex-

Priscilla was sitting in her wheelchair when Carrie, Lester and Michael passed by.

plained reasonably, and Michael turned in the doorway and asked, 'Why can't Bristler be seen to?'

'Bristler?'

'He can't say Priscilla.' Lester again explained the obvious.

'We've done all we can,' the mother said curtly.

Outside in the wheelchair, the little girl sat with her mittened hands limp on the rug over her knees, staring without expression into the room.

Before they crossed the road into the stubble field, Carrie, Lester and Michael rode round the high garden hedge to the back gate for one more look at Priscilla.

The father had gone out to bring her in. He had turned the chair round to pull it backwards over the door sill. John, who was anxious to get home, tossed his brown head over the gate. Oliver stuck his furry nose through the bars to bite at a bush. It tasted bitter, and he snorted smoky breath into the cold air.

The father was turned to the door and did not see the horses. But in the moment before he pulled her after him, Priscilla came to life. The dark eyes brightened. The limp hands lifted to clutch the arms of the wheelchair and pull herself forward. Her still, pale face moved into a smile, just for a moment, before the chair was jerked inside and the door shut.

Five

Every day in his plaid dressing gown, Jerome Fielding threw away the pages he had written the day before and started again. It was going to be a long time before they all became rich and famous.

27

Every evening, Em collected the crumpled paper from under the table, smoothed it out and wrote some more of her play in bed by the stub of a candle, wearing moth-eaten gloves with no fingers.

It was a play about herself as she would like to be, tall and willowy with a face like a lily, long straight cornsilk hair, and a beautiful singing voice, honest and courageous and adored. It was called *Life and Death of a Star*. Would it make anybody rich and famous? Perhaps she would never show it to anyone.

When Mother had finished darning clothes and pruning fruit trees and painting Liza's bedstead bright orange daisies on the corners, she went chatting round the villages to see what was doing.

'What *was* doing?' When she came home, Carrie and Michael were washing a horse rug in the sink, and Dad had some of the dogs lined up like sailors on pay day to catch dog biscuits.

Moses caught them in his long speckled jaws like an alligator. Liza's old dog Dusty would not open his mouth at all. The biscuit bumped off his faded nose and he had to track it short-sightedly over the floor. Harry, silly half-brother of Moses, snapped wildly, jumping too high and slavering. Charlie didn't bother to open his mouth until the last minute, then he caught the biscuit neatly and casually over his shoulder.

'What *was* doing, Alice?'

'The assistant cook at the school is leaving to have a baby. I may get the job.'

'Now look here, Alice.' Someone's puppy flopped on to Dad's foot and he flipped it off upside down, its legs bicycling round its fat stomach. 'I'm not going to have you breaking your back.'

'I've done that once and it mended.' Mother laughed and swung her yellow bell of hair, excited by the future. She lived in the expectation that something marvellous was just round the corner. Anything new, even boiling up carrots and jam roll for a hundred and fifty messy, grumbling children, was an adventure. 'Let me do this, just till you get some money for the book.'

'Ah – and then you shall live like a lady. Jewels. Furs. Exotic perfumes. Champagne ...'

'I don't want to live like a lady.' Mother kicked off her shoes and sat on the draining board to wash her feet in the horse rug water.

'She'd give the jewels to the poor,' Michael said.

'And furs come from endangered species,' Carrie said.

'And exoct pre-fumes are made from the insides of cats,' Michael said.

'What about champagne then?'

They were stumped for a moment, then Carrie grinned and shouted, 'Picking the grapes is cruel to the birds!' and Charlie shouted with her.

By opening his mouth wide and using a lot of breath, he could make sounds like loud talking, as long as you didn't want consonants.

Dad threw him a biscuit, which he caught back and sideways with a flick of his head.

'Well fielded, sir!'

'If the balls weren't so hard,' Michael said, 'he could play for England.'

Actually, Charlie was not much good at balls. If you threw one for him, he either looked the wrong way, or took it under a bush and demolished it. When he went with Carrie and Lester and Michael on a further Brookside reconnaissance at halfterm, a tennis ball came sailing over the garden hedge as they were riding at the edge of the field behind the house. Charlie pounced on it and ran into the bushes.

Michael got off his pony and crawled in after him. Charlie's jaws were clamped round a brand new ball. Michael got it out by putting a finger inside and tickling the roof of his mouth. He stood up to throw the ball over the hedge, but it went behind his head into the field. After two more tries, he turned round and lobbed it backwards over the hedge and into the Brookside garden.

Crash – clatter – tinkle. Yells from beyond the hedge. Michael dropped to hands and knees and peered through.

'Straight into a cold frame.' He backed out of the hedge with the shoulder of his jacket half torn away. 'What did I tell you? Two broken windows always means a third.'

They went round to the back gate. A hefty boy and girl in shorts much too cold for this weather were jumping about on the tennis court waving racquets and shouting, 'Thanks for the ball!'

They did not seem to mind about the cold frame. But Michael would not go in alone, so Carrie went with him while Lester held the horses.

The boy and girl were as strong and healthy as their parents, with brown limbs, thick shiny hair, red lips over big white teeth and large rubber-soled feet. They looked like the super-young of a new vitamin-stuffed race. Very different from the little girl who sat bundled in a cape and hood in the doorway of the round summerhouse, her skinny legs dangling into boots that hung uselessly.

She sat in her own world. When Michael waved to her, she did not smile, but slid her eyes round to where the boy and girl were hanging like apes against the wire fence of the tennis court.

'I'm Victor Agnew.' The boy grinned, sure of himself and of being liked. 'And this is Jane. Who are you?'

'We broke your cold frame,' Carrie said. Michael had pulled his hood down over his eyes which meant that he was not going to speak.

'Oh that.' The boy tossed back a lion's mane of hair, as if cold frames came two a penny. 'What have you got out there – horses?'

'Do you ride?' Carrie asked eagerly. The boy looked her age, or a bit older. Lester was all the friend she needed, of course, but fantasy catapulted her forward into a dream of riding with this boy, dazzling him with how well John went for her.

The boy and girl dropped their monkey grins for a moment and shot a look at each other. Then the boy made a

30

noise of contempt and pushed himself off the wire. 'Who wants a horse when they can go by car?'

'We don't have time to play about with ponies.' The girl recovered her grin. 'Games is our thing. Want to come and knock up?' She picked up her racquet and banged some balls across the net, hard enough to stop a train.

'We don't play.'

'Don't play *tennis*?' Carrie might as well have said, 'We don't eat.'

'What's going on out there, you kids? I said three sets before lunch if you want to win that tournament.' The father bounced out of the house in swimming trunks with a towel round his broad bare shoulders.

Swimming in the winter! Carrie and Michael stared. They spent a lot of their winter trying to get warm or keep warm, not cooling off in cold water. The pool had been repaired and filled. There seemed to be a thin skin of ice in one corner.

Poised on the edge, the large red-faced man threw off the towel, flexed his muscles, did a few Tarzan knee bends, and plunged into the icy water. Carrie could feel the shock of it through all her nerves and up into her head, where it made her teeth ache.

The man did not reappear immediately. She almost expected to see him float to the top dead, with the red broken veins of his face congealed to blue, but he swam underwater and surfaced at the other end of the pool, flinging back his hair and jumping half out of the water as if he hoped to be thrown a herring. He swam several lengths in a powerful crawl, hauled himself easily out of the pool, wiped his hands over his eyes and saw Michael goggling at him.

'You again,' he said. 'What do you want?'

'Oh, they're our friends,' Victor called out from the court, as if the whole world was his friend once it had spoken to him.

'Make yourselves at home then.' Mr Agnew slung the towel round his neck, put up his elbows and jogged across the terrace into the house. Carrie distinctly saw gooseflesh on the backs of his legs.

She tested the water in the pool and almost got frost-bitten fingers. Victor and Jane had finished their game and were coming through the gate of the court.

'Does your father swim all winter?' she asked them.

'Natch. Got to keep fit, you know, at his age, or you go to seed. He jogs two miles every day. So do we when we're home from school. What's your name?'

'I'm Caroline,' Carrie heard herself say, although she never used her full name. 'And my brother is Michael.'

The girl had run towards the house. Victor turned towards the summer-house.

'Come on Priskie, old sport.' He grabbed the handle at the back of the little girl's chair and bumped her off the step on to the path so vigorously that she nearly fell out.

'Can I push her?' Michael walked beside him with the slight limp that made him look as if he had one foot on the pavement and one in the gutter.

'Help yourself. I get enough of it.'

'What's wrong with Priscilla?' The boy was so cheerful and relaxed that Carrie was able to ask it.

'Old Priskie? She's all right.'

'Why do you all say that?' This boy seemed so direct and easygoing, and yet here he was, lying like his parents.

'What do you want us to say – that she's a hopeless cripple who'll never walk again?' He kept smiling, but he banged his tennis racquet savagely against a juniper bush.

'Oh.'

'Her spinal cord was injured. Her pony reared and fell back on top of her.'

'I'm sorry.' Carrie did not look at him either. 'I shouldn't have asked you if you rode.'

'Oh, *we* never did. Priskie was the horsy one. She'd have won at all the shows. That stinking pony cost the earth.'

'Was it too much for such a small child?'

32

'Look – she was more than seven,' Victor said scornfully, as if Carrie should have known that all Agnews were champs as soon as they could toddle.

'How old is she now?'

'About nine.' Didn't people in wheelchairs have birthdays?

'She doesn't look it.'

'She's gone babyish.'

'Who says she'll never walk?'

'Everyone. She might have. But she wouldn't try. She won't do exercises or anything. She's given up.'

They had been walking towards the house, thinking that Michael was walking behind them with the rapt, careful face he had put on when he took charge of the wheelchair. But when they reached the terrace and Victor turned to help lift the chair up the steps, they saw that Michael had gone in the other direction, and had taken Priscilla to the back gate to see the horses.

He had opened the gate and pushed her through.

'My mother will burst a blood vessel. Hey, Ma!' Victor ran across the terrace, Carrie turned and ran to the gate, and the mother came hurtling out of the house behind her with a cry.

Outside the back gate, the chair was bogged in winter mud. Michael held Oliver close to it and had picked up Priscilla's small hand and pulled it forward. The child showed no fear. Her grave eyes watched the pony's full blue eye.

'Let him smell you, Bristler.' Michael pulled off the woollen mitten and held her hand against the soft twitching nose. Oliver liked the smell of people. He blew curious breaths into the tiny hand, white and fragile against Michael's blunt brown workman's fingers.

'Horses smell by breathing out, not in,' Michael instructed Priscilla chummily.

'Yes.' It was only a whisper, but it was the first word she had said.

Her mother had no breath to shout. With a sobbing gasp,

she came through the gate and snatched the child up out of the chair and held her close, boots dangling at the end of the wrinkled red tights. Priscilla began to put on the high baby wailing they had heard before. Over her mother's shoulder, her face was screwed up fretfully, but with no tears.

'What are you trying to do?' Mrs Agnew asked Michael angrily.

'She likes the horses, really she does.'

'She's terrified of them.' The mother had backed away to the gate, as if she were the one who was terrified. 'You must leave her alone. I told you.'

'She's lonely.'

'She wants to be alone. She doesn't like other children. Leave her alone – please!' as Michael reached up to put the mitten on the dangling hand. 'Don't upset her.'

Carrying the light weight of the child easily against her strong shoulder, she went through the gate. Carrie began to follow with the chair, but she said, 'Leave that. I'll send Victor out for it.'

They watched her stride back with the wailing child across the garden and into the house and shut the door.

Six

The big stubble field had been ploughed now. They picked their way along the sticky outside furrow in single file, not talking. When they got on to the broad track through the wood, Lester rode up beside Carrie.

'Victor,' he said. 'How do you like that?'

Carrie shrugged her shoulders.

'It means Conqueror.' Lester's mother had a book of names, which she consulted whenever a relation or friend was going to have a baby, and handed out advice which they never took.

'Well, he seems to be always winning at games.'

'All brawn and no brain. I know his sort.'

Lester was jealous, but Carrie was thinking about the little girl. 'He said it was an expensive show pony. Perhaps the mother bought something much too hot for her because the family always has to win.'

'So that makes her think it's her fault,' Michael jogged alongside. Because he did not read or write what the school called properly, they said he was backward, but he was very shrewd for his age.

'That's why she babies Priscilla,' Lester said. 'She didn't start crying till Mrs Agnew came on the scene.'

'Mrs Agony,' Michael said. 'She's made a prisoner of Bristler.'

Late that night, Carrie was thinking about Priscilla lying perhaps in that spooky round turret room at Brookside, and unable to go to the curved window and look out at the cold moon and the bare trees weaving changing designs on the night sky in the same breeze that blew the curtain into Carrie's room, even though the window was shut.

Did she know that the house was haunted? The other Agnews did not look as if they would believe a ghost if they met one head on. If they should hear the phantom baby crying, they would think it was Priscilla's desolate wail.

And *was* it Priscilla she and Lester had heard that day in the turret room? Or was it . . . ?

To stop herself thinking about ghosts when everyone else was asleep in the quiet house, Carrie lit a candle and called Perpetua up on to the feed sacks stuffed with Henry's last shearing, which was her quilt. Always having puppies was making Perpetua broader. Her back made a good prop for the notebook in which Carrie made her entries for *Carrie's Horse Book*.

Remembering how Priscilla and Oliver had begun to

communicate without words before the mother rushed up, she wrote:

A horse blows out to smell not by sniffing in.

If you let him blow into your hand, he will know you.

A horse talks with breath.

A horse brain weighs $1\frac{1}{4}$ lb. A human brain weighs 3 lb. If people have more brains, why don't they try to understand what a horse says instead of expecting him to understand what they say?

'He understands every word I say. He's almost human,' they say.

He is not human. He is a horse.

But he is more intelligent because he understands Walk on, and Trot, and Canter, and Whoa, and knows his own name.

People don't understand when he says, I'm frightened, and they don't even want to know what name a horse calls them.

Carrie knew what John called her. He called her 'She', using it as a name.

When the candle blew out in the draught and she lay with her book and pencil fallen to the floor and Perpetua a dead weight on her legs, the brown horse came to her window and called, 'She-ee-ee!' in the soft high whinny no one else could hear.

She closed her eyes and together they galloped up to the Elysian Star where famous horses grazed, and horses who were waiting for their people to die and join them. A bow-legged Spanish gipsy was sitting on the gate watching a rickety old donkey weave its way through the grass to him, with hips like coat hangers and its ears sticking through holes in a straw hat.

Some of the thoroughbreds, who were pretty conceited, were calling to the gipsy, 'Get a horse!' which was what carriage horses from the early days of motoring used to call out as they passed drivers whose cars had broken down.

One of the jokers was a very beautiful bay pony mare, nervous and quick. She went off like a rocket when the donkey suddenly let out a bray like a rusty opera singer being strangled on the high note.

It was the show pony that had reared backwards with Priscilla.

'Don't blame me,' she said, flicking her delicate ears as the gipsy hung a necklace with bells on the donkey and led it through the gate. 'I was jittery as hell. They'd over-schooled and overfed me. Pep drugs too.'

'You die of an overdose?' John asked.

'After the accident, they had me destroyed. Fair enough. The insurance money paid some of the doctors. I like it better up here anyway. No horse shows.'

The next day, Carrie met Victor Agnew in the iron-monger's, where she had gone to try to barter ducks' eggs for paraffin.

Victor was buying linseed oil for his hibernating cricket bat and dubbin for his football boots. His highly coloured health and loud clear voice filled the cluttered little shop which smelled of turpentine and firewood, and made the old ladies waiting for clothes pins and potato peelers look very small and grey.

When Carrie asked him if the show pony had been destroyed, he said, 'No fear. They sold it for more than they gave.'

So much for the Star.

Seven

Mother got the job as assistant cook at the school. She could usually get herself into any job by bluffing, though she couldn't always hold it when they found out she didn't know as much as she pretended.

When they asked her if she had had a lot of experience in cooking for large numbers, she said Yes, and went away and bought a book, *Quantity Cooking for Institutions*.

'Quaintly Cooking of Instruments.' Michael picked it up. 'School dinners will be weirder than ever.'

He left the book in the barn and Lucy the Nubian goat ate it, so Mother had to learn on the job.

Since there was no room for her to go to school in the trap behind John, she bought a spindly-looking bicycle called Spider Monkey, with spokes that got loose and gouged your ankles, and a little two-stroke motor that sounded like the first internal combustion engine ever built.

She bought it on credit from Mr Peasly's son at the garage, so when Dad protested about the job, she was able to say she must stick to it until she had paid for the bicycle.

She had to be in the school kitchen early to get the vegetables peeled, so she went off with the others, putt-putting through the lanes alongside John's steady clip-clip. They were quiet roads that took them to the school. As soon as they got through the village and past the policeman's house, Mother would get into the trap and let Carrie or Em or Michael ride Spider Monkey.

It wouldn't go very fast, but the engine was so noisy and the frame so clacketty that it felt like speeding. Michael made himself a pair of goggles out of the rims of jar lids and blue cellophane from a bar of soap, and put an enamel bowl inside his hood to make it a crash helmet.

Carrie rode crouched over the handlebars like a jockey.

When the petrol ran out, which it usually did on the way home because the tank leaked, she hung on to the shaft of the trap and let John pull her and the bicycle along.

Em rode with her father's old beret jammed on her curls and refused to get off when it was the end of her turn.

It actually took longer than before to get to school, because they had to keep stopping and changing places and fighting about whose turn it was. Their names were often written in the Late Book and Mrs Reeper, who was producing the Christmas play, told Em that if she was late for one more rehearsal, she might miss her chance to play the angel.

One morning when there was an early rehearsal, they were later than ever. Everything at home had held them up. A cat had a piece of broken glass in its foot, growling neurotically and needing two people to hold it and one with the tweezers. One of Michael's boots totally vanished. Another cat stole the bacon, and the last of the milk was spilled. The ribbon snake which Tom was foster-mothering escaped up a drainpipe. Liza had one of her fits in which anything a grown up said was provoking, even Good Morning.

'It's not good,' she sulked, eating round the crusts of her toast like a child. 'It's pouring rain. It's not morning either. It's the middle of the night.'

It was one of those dark grey winter mornings when the sun has not bothered to come up since it will soon be time to go down again.

'What a rotten life. Being dragged out of bed to get that stinking bus to that lousy job.'

'I thought you liked working for Mr Harvey.' Mother was at the sink, scraping toast over the front of her white school overall.

'Work's a dirty word to me.'

'Yes dear,' Mother said, not really listening.

But Liza snapped, 'You calling me lazy? All right, I'll go.' World's End was her home, but she and her mother had spent so many years shouting abuse at each other that

39

Liza sometimes had to exercise her tongue muscles, like a horse bucking and kicking when you turn it out. 'Been here too long anyway, me and Dusty.'

'Don't talk to Alice like that.' Jerome Fielding appeared in pyjamas and a fisherman's jersey.

'Oh, don't *you* get into it,' Liza said, as rudely as if she were his own daughter.

She banged out, and he asked mildly, 'Did I smell bacon, Alice?'

Carrie was late getting John into the trap, because a buckle broke and had to be mended with a leather shoelace. Mother couldn't get Spider Monkey to start until the trap had pulled her a few hundred yards down the lane, hanging on to the end of a halter rope like a water skier.

When they were past the yellow brick house where Constable Dunstable lived, Mother got off the bicycle and Em jumped out of the trap.

'It's not your turn.' Michael got down, adjusting his jarlid goggles.

'Mrs Reeper said if I was late again I couldn't be in the play.'

Em had the important part of the angel on top of the Christmas tree, who saves the toys from a burglar by stabbing him with her wand. Everyone was coming to watch it, even Dad. He had never been to the school, and people said the Fieldings had made him up. But he was coming to watch Em be the star of the play.

'I'm going to ride ahead.' Em got on to the bicycle seat and tried to pry Michael's fingers off the handlebars. Chug-chug went the little motor on the back wheel. Em suddenly put it in gear, opened the throttle and knocked Michael sprawling in the road.

'Watch the brakes!' Mum called after her, but Em had her head down to the rain and the beret jammed over her ears, putta-putta-putting noisily up the hill with a cloud of blue smoke behind her.

Spider Monkey slowed going up the curves of the hill, but picked up again as they went through the fir wood at

Em sprawled into the grass at the side of the road.

the top, with the trees not sheltering, but chucking wind-blown branchfuls of water down Em's back. She was soaked through. When she got to the warm gym where they rehearsed, she would steam.

Down the long white hill into the small town where the school was, the bicycle went as fast as flying. With the wind and the rain, Em could hardly see. When the yellow tractor loomed suddenly ahead, dragging a lifted rake, she jammed on the feeble brakes, then turned the handlebars just in time before she crashed into the iron teeth of the rake.

Spider Monkey skidded on the wet chalky surface, the wheels slid sideways and Em sprawled into the grass at the side of the road with her books spilled out of her satchel into the ditch.

The tractor made more noise than the bicycle. Having heard nothing, the driver went his dignified way down the hill.

Em got up. She could not let the others come trotting out of the trees at the top of the hill and find her like this. The front of the bicycle frame was jammed, but if she ran across the fields, she might just get to school before the end of the rehearsal.

She stuffed her books back into her satchel, dragged Spider Monkey through a gateway and behind a hedge so that the others would not see, and set off running across a meadow where a dozen cows were lying down to keep a bit of grass dry to eat when the rain stopped. Chewing cuds, they didn't even look round to watch her go by.

Through the fence at the other end, splashing across a track pitted with puddles, Em skirted round the back of a house, and a dog flew out of a kennel to bite her leg. She swerved. The dog was brought up short by a chain and his jaws snapped air.

A window at the back of the house went up and a head in pink rollers yelled, 'Get out of there!'

Em got. Over a wall, down an alley, running across a timber yard, limping out into the High Street after she knocked her ankle on the corner edge of a plank.

The church clock said eight thirty-five. Rehearsals started at eight-thirty. Em ran on down the street, but her breath was rasping and her legs felt as if they were going in slow motion, like a dream when you can only run on the same spot.

A woman with an umbrella grabbed her by the pillar box.

'Esmeralda!' It was Mrs Nixon, for whom she had baby-sat. 'Where are you going in such a state?'

'I—I—' Em started wildly, but had no breath to speak.

'You're early for school anyway. Come inside and dry off. You're all wet and muddy. I'll lend you one of Tommy's jackets. Whatever happened?' She took Em inside her house and into the kitchen.

'I fell off my mother's bike.'

'That noisy thing that smells up the street? You shouldn't be riding that anyway at your age.'

She went out of the kitchen. Was she going to tell the police?

Em went through what she thought was the back door, remembering too late that it wasn't, and found herself in a dark pantry, just as Mrs. Nixon came back into the kitchen saying, 'Esmeralda, here's a warm— Gone. Well, how do you like that? That's the way they are these days, the young people.'

She muttered round the kitchen, while Em crouched beside a pickle crock under a shelf and heard a kettle whistle, clatter of china, and the radio, as Mrs Nixon sat herself down to a cup of tea.

In the dark under the pantry shelf, Em saw in the eye of her mind the stage of the gym lit with coloured lights, herself on the stepladder behind the tree, holding her wand with the star, a gold ribbon round her hair and her face angelic, her father in the audience grinning round proudly to make sure everybody knew she was his daughter.

'Now while the children sleep on Christmas Eve,
The toys are wide awake, you must believe.

43

Now while the white Frost King rides through the night...'

The larder window was very narrow, but Em was a narrow person. Somehow she managed to climb on to the top shelf and open the lock and squeeze herself through. She tore her anorak and the beret fell into a lidless dustbin, but Em was free.

She raced down the street, across the playground and down the passage to the gym.

'Walk, don't run, dear.' Miss de Witt passed with her silly smile and her head on one side from draughts in the art studio.

Em slowed round a corner, then ran again and burst into the gym.

They were all on the stage. Three small ones who played the children were crosslegged on the floor. The toys were in a heap, scrapping and giggling. The candles were standing straight and bored with their hands at their sides. On the stepladder, ugly, ugly with that hair like frayed rope—

'Oh there you are, Em. You look as if you'd swum here.' Mrs Reeper, who acted with the local Drama Society, gave her tinkly stage laugh.

'Sorry I'm late.' Em stared at Sonia Jenks on the stepladder.

'It doesn't matter. I was going to tell you anyway, Mrs Loomis wants more music, so we've had to make the angel into a solo singing part.'

Em couldn't carry a tune in a bucket. Everyone knew that. When there was a solo it was always Sonia, with that freak high voice from blocked sinuses.

'You'll still be in the play, of course,' Mrs Reeper said. 'I want you to be one of my good red candles.'

A *candle*. The dopes and dodos were candles.

'You can have the costume my mother made,' Sonia said in that voice as if she had a clothes peg on the top of her nose.

'I won't be here.'

'Now Em, just because you can't have the main part. It's the show that matters, you know. The play's the thing.'

'I'm going away with my father.'

'Where to?'

'Switzerland.'

'Lucky you,' Mrs Reeper said in her flutey acting voice that did not show whether she believed it or not.

Nobody understood the size of the disaster.

Mother said, 'What a shame. But I'd have been proud of you as a candle anyway, especially if I didn't have to make the costume.' It was all right for her. She'd had her day on the stage before Dad took her off it to the altar.

Carrie said, 'That stupid play, you're well out of *that*.' It was all right for her. She'd almost won the jumping at the horse show, and she'd saved the stolen dogs and been a heroine. Got almost killed too. If Em got completely killed, then they would pay attention. *We never appreciated her.* She could see the funeral.

Her father said, 'Thank God, now I shan't have to go to the school.'

Michael said, 'Silly old Sonia. Silly old Mrs Creeper.' He wasn't even angry with Em for pushing him into the road. 'Em's like that,' he said.

I'm not. She wrote the whole thing into her play, with a character like Sonia Jenks having the accident, and the heroine, who was her understudy, becoming a star over-night.

When the play was produced, when she was famous, then they'd all be sorry.

Eight

Spider Monkey would cost about £5 to repair.

'I'll pay,' Em said, after she and her mother had left the bicycle at Dick Peasly's garage.

'You needn't.'

'Let me.'

'All right.' Mother knew when it was all right to take your money, and when it wasn't.

Em had a bit of cash in her bank, which was a hole hollowed out of the plaster behind a torn patch of wallpaper in her room. And she would make bird feeders and sell them as Christmas presents. Miss Etty, in the bungalow built round the tree, had a special way of making cat-proof feeders. Although cats came first with Em and she always sided with them, even after a slaughter, she compensated by making places for the birds to feed in safety.

Carrie and Michael said they would help, to get Spider Monkey back on the road, so they all went to tea with Miss Etty.

She gave them lardy cake made of a fatty dough with currants and crystals of sugar. It was the last sort of food she needed, mountainous as she was, but the birds liked it. She always baked things that birds especially liked.

Perched among the bare branches of the tree that grew slantwise through a corner of her living-room were a moth-eaten old starling that had lived with her for as long as she could remember, some sparrows, and a thrush that was wintering here instead of farther south. On the circular table built round the tree trunk, was a crow that Miss Etty had found with two broken legs. She had kept him propped in a box of dry grass, and though the bones had never mended strongly, he had grown callouses on his elbows, so he could hop or sit on them with his claws in the air. His name was Albert and he was clever, like all crows. A scarecrow is fooling itself if it thinks it can fool a crow.

He could mimic sounds, including the winter wheezing of Miss Etty's jumbo chest. They say that people get to look like their animals, but Miss Etty wasn't anything like a bird. She was as big as two people, and always sat on the couch, since she overlapped the chairs. Lester said they had built the bungalow round her as well as the tree, and then had to widen the doorways because she couldn't get out.

She wore long skirts made of curtains, so that you could only guess from an occasional glimpse of a massive ankle at the size of her legs. Her round chins were uncountable, and her cushiony hands were short-fingered, like paws.

But she used them skilfully. When they had finished the cake, and the thrush and sparrows had polished off the currants and crumbs, including the ones on Michael's chin, she showed them how to take an empty soup tin and knot odd ends of string to make a net round it. You then slipped out the tin and kept it by your kitchen sink and put into it every bit of bacon grease and rind, fat off plates, vegetable scraps, breadcrumbs, potato, damp dog biscuit. You mixed in peanut butter and oatmeal and sunflower seeds as you went along and when it was full and the fat congealed, you cut out the other end and pushed the cylinder of bird food out into the tin-sized net.

You threaded string through the top, with long ends to hang it far enough from a branch to be safe from cats, wrapped it in red cellophane, tied it with a bow made from a bright piece in the rag bag, and Lo, you had a Christmas gift you could sell house-to-house and make almost a hundred per cent profit.

While they were knotting nets round the cans, Miss Etty sat with a bird in her hair and another on her huge thumb pulling ends of string out of her fist. A bird called outside and Theo the thrush in her hair lifted his head and answered, 'Cheerily, cheerily.'

Em said, 'He's saying, "This room is mine." '

'The other one's saying. "Then stay out of my tree,"' Carrie said.

'He's calling "Danger from cats,"' Michael said. 'I saw Caesar following us in the long grass.'

'He's saying, "I'm Lester Figg, trying to sound like a robin."' Miss Etty found some cake in the pocket of a tooth and chumped her comfortable dewlaps. 'He can fool Theo, but he doesn't fool me.'

'How did you know we were here?' Carrie opened the wide back door. Lester wasn't there.

'I am the All-seeing Eye.' He was in the branches of the tree where it grew out of the roof.

'You asked at my house.'

'I haven't been there.' He jumped down. 'I've been at Brookside. Keeping watch.'

When there was an interesting situation, Lester kept watch silently, like an Indian. Most of what he knew he had learned by watching and listening. He had once overheard three men behind a hoarding plotting to rob a bank. Instead of telling the police or the bank manager, he had hidden in a dustbin all one freezing night and got pneumonia. But the bank was not robbed, which proved either that he had foiled the three men, or imagined them.

'How's Bristler?' Michael tightened the last knot with his teeth and drew out the soup tin.

'Abandoned.'

'To her fate?' Michael leaned across the table with his eyes bulging and his jaw open. The sparrow who was pecking at the string flew on to his shoulder and very delicately picked a lardy cake crumb from the corner of his mouth.

'Not quite. She's been left with a keeper. The Agnews have gone to Old Boys' weekend at Victor's school. Mr Agnew is playing rugger for the Old Boys.'

'He would,' Carrie said.

'Don't be narrow,' Miss Etty said sharply. 'Everyone can't have your advantages. Have you heard the ghost yet?' she asked Lester.

'We've heard ... things.'

'A baby?' Her shrewd black eyes looked at him sideways over the hills of her cheeks.

'Perhaps.' Miss Etty loved mysteries, so he didn't tell her it could have been Priscilla.

'The poor little baby ... yes ... yes ...' Miss Etty nodded, as if she were remembering. 'A hundred years ago or more, it must have been. My grandmother told me. Our family used to live in that village, you know, in the mill cottage, until the damp of the stream got to my grandmother. Then my mother. I was the first one had the sense to move.'

'What did your grandmother tell you?' They had stopped working to watch her. Theo went to sleep in her hair. Lester picked up the crippled crow and perched on the table round the tree trunk, stroking him with one finger.

'Long, long ago, it was. Long before Brookside was built. They didn't know about old Diller, or they'd never have built that fancy house there where the spinney used to be.'

'Who was old Diller?' Michael hardly dared ask it. He loved horror stories and dreaded them at the same time.

'He was a batty old character, had to do everything different from other people. In those days, it was horses and carts, but Diller had three big dogs and he harnessed them to a home-made wagon. Three abreast, the dogs used to dash him along the highway. Horses would shy and coachmen used to give him the horn. Daft Diller, they called him. At the inns, they wouldn't serve him, or feed the dogs.'

'Poor Diller,' Em said.

'Even his wife had deserted him. Jealous of the dogs, so the story goes. But there was one thing old Diller wanted in life, and that was a child. A child who would remember him, and look after his dogs when he was gone.

'There was a woman had a baby and she didn't want it, which is one of the worst things that can happen to a baby, so don't try it next time you're born. She used to keep it in the wash house because she couldn't stand it crying, and one night, daft Diller stole it away, all bundled up and probably crying to raise the dead, but the mother snored on with her nightcap over her ears.

'Diller put it into the cart with him, gave his team the order and away they went. They were coming across the fields there, back of where Brookside is now, heading for the only bridge there was in those days, to cross the stream. There must have been a rabbit ran into the spinney, because those big dogs went after it, dashing old Diller and his wagon and his baby in among the trees.'

Miss Etty paused, heaving and wheezing.

'Go on.'

But she could only flap a pudgy hand at Michael, trying to get her breath. Em went into the kitchen and came back with a bottle of vinegar which she held under Miss Etty's nose, and she sniffed it mightily.

'Thank you.' Her chest stopped heaving. Her wobbling cheeks and chins grew still. Her eyes cleared. Theo, who had been roving restlessly in her hair during the commotion, settled down again.

'It was the crying of the baby that led them to find him. Daft Diller was dead, his skull bashed against a tree. One of his dogs was dead too, choked itself trying to struggle free of the harness. The other two had bitten through the leather straps and gone. The baby was lying bundled up among the splinters of the wagon.'

'What happened to it?'

'No one knew. The only thing they did know was that sometimes after that, people going by the spinney would hear a wailing. They began to cut down the trees to try and put a stop to it. But one of the woodmen heard the barking of dogs. Dogs that weren't there. And the other – the other, when he struck his axe into a young tree, it sobbed like an infant. They ran, both of them.'

'So would I.'

'It wasn't till many years afterwards when the land was sold and that house Brookside was to be built, that the trees were cut down by machinery saws, too loud to hear the baby or the dogs.'

'We heard them.'

'I told you.' Miss Etty nodded at Lester. 'I told you, didn't I? You can change the scenery all you want, build a house, tear down a monastery, to the dead it stays the same. There's a house in Rutland where they raised the floor to put in heating pipes, and the ghost of the grey lady walks through on her knees, because she's walking where the old floor was.'

'When we were in the turret room ...' Carrie remembered how Lester had listened to the wind. 'But we thought it was dogs barking.'

'We thought it was Bristler crying,' Michael said.

'There's some people hear ghosts,' Miss Etty said, 'and some that don't.'

Nine

There was no question where they should go on Saturday.

It was an unexpectedly warm day – hooray for Mr Agnew and his Old Boys' rugger – so they would ride over to Brookside, and take halters to tie up the horses.

'Why don't you go in the trap so I can come?' Em asked.

'Why don't you ride Leonora?'

'She goes in circles, Carrie, you know she does.'

'Only because you don't know how to ride donkeys. Why don't you learn to ride properly?'

'Why should I? Lester doesn't.'

'Lester rides by instinct.' Carrie had given up trying to teach him the correct way. And if you rode Peter in a saddle and bridle, collected, using the aids of hands and legs, his old bad experiences came back to him and he went berserk.

'Ride Old Red then,' Carrie suggested.

Old Red was the clanking conglomeration of crimson-painted iron on which Liza rode to catch the bus every morning. It was so old, it still had a net skirt-guard on the back wheel from the days when ladies wore long skirts. Now that they did again, Liza rode the bicycle in her long hooded maxi-coat over her blue jeans, pedalling into the misted morning beechwoods like a witch.

'Liza's gone off on the bike,' Em said. 'She's got a boyfriend.'

'She hasn't.' Liza was so rude to boys, she never had a boyfriend. She had promised to marry Michael.

'When I asked her where she was going, she yelled at me to mind my own business,' Em said. 'So it must be a boy. I don't want to come anyway,' she added, since Carrie and Lester didn't want her. They only took Michael because he was part of the riding thing.

She sat by the stove and unravelled a scarf to make knitting wool. When her father, coming in for coffee with a pencil stuck through his beard, asked, 'Why didn't you go out with the others on this good day?' she said, 'I didn't want to.'

Priscilla was in the garden in her chair on the summerhouse step, staring listlessly at the cold blue water of the swimming pool.

Her keeper, a middle-aged woman in the hat and dark blue uniform of a District Nurse, sat on a bench nearby, reading a book with gloves on.

Carrie, Lester and Michael came through the back gate.

'Who are you?' The nurse looked up, narrowing her eyes shortsightedly over a thin red nose and chapped lips.

'We're friends of the family.' Boldness was best.

'We heard they were away,' Michael said, 'so we came to keep Bristler company.'

'Priscilla?' The nurse frowned and glanced towards the child in the wheelchair.

'I'll push her round the garden a bit. Give her a change of scene.'

Michael started towards Priscilla, but the nurse reached forward and grabbed him. 'No one is to bother her. I've had strict orders.'

'She's lonely.' Michael sat on the bench and swung his feet.

'I daresay she is, poor little soul, but that's what her mother wants, and I'm paid to follow orders, not think for myself.'

She must be very limited as a nurse. What would she do alone with a life-or-death patient, and no one there to do the thinking?

Lester sat down on the other side of her. 'Why don't you go in out of the cold? We'll watch Priscilla.'

'I'm to stay with her.'

'Let's take her into the house then. I'll wheel her.' Lester was dying to get back into the turret room.

'She's to stay outside for exactly two hours.' The nurse pushed back her glove to look at her watch. 'Another forty minutes.'

Michael tried again. 'She's tired of looking at all that ugly cold water.'

'A swimming pool is nice,' the nurse said vaguely.

'If you can swim in it. Drusilla can't. I can't either. I nearly drowned once,' Michael began chattily, but the nurse was picking chapped skin off her lips, not interested.

It was Carrie's turn to try. 'Coming through the village,' she said, 'I heard people saying there was a woman going to have a baby. We could stay with Priscilla if you want to go and check.'

'Nurse Duggan will be sent for. I'm retired now, you see.' The sun travelled cheerfully out of a cloud and when she looked up at it, they saw that her cold dry skin was cracked into elderly lines. 'I still wear the uniform though. It makes me feel more workmanlike.'

'Doesn't it make Priscilla feel like a patient?' Lester asked.

'Well, she is a patient, isn't she?' The nurse had shut the book, quite glad of a chance to talk instead of read.

'But perhaps she just feels like an ordinary child.'

'How can she?' She turned her head to Michael. 'She's handicapped.'

The nurse spoke quite loudly, and when Carrie, Lester and Michael looked to see if Priscilla had heard, she said, 'Oh, don't worry. She's quite retarded too, I think.'

'What's that mean?'

She looked at Michael and tapped her forehead.

'Why?' Lester asked.

'She hardly speaks.' The nurse had to keep swivelling from Michael to Lester and back again. 'Or takes notice of you. Then the infantile way she cries. I heard her last night, but when I went to her room, there was nothing wrong.'

'Perhaps it wasn't her crying,' Lester said softly.

'What do you mean?' The nurse looked behind her, as if her spine had just crept away. 'There's no one else in the house.'

'Except the ghost.'

'Ghost, what ghost?' She fidgeted. 'Don't be ridiculous, there's no such thing as ghosts.' She suddenly let out a small shriek, as if she had seen one. 'Get away from there, you brute!'

Charlie had finished blazing the trail of a lifted leg all over the Agnews' garden, and wandered over to investigate Priscilla. He was usually shy of new people, but he put his rough head on the rug that covered her knees. Slowly and jerkily, she brought a hand out from under the rug and buried it in his long hair. He sat down and leaned against the chair.

'You see,' Carrie said. 'It's all right.'

'The Agnews don't like animals.'

'Oh well, Charlie doesn't mind.'

Lester began to tell the nurse the story of old Diller: 'Daft Diller they called him, and he stole this woman's baby.' But she opened her book again and said, 'Don't bother me.'

'The baby has been heard,' Lester said. 'And the barking of the dogs too.'

As if he heard them, Charlie stood up and lifted his tufted ears square to his head. His tail was curled on to his back in the mongrel giveaway that would have sent his golden retriever father into sixty fits.

'What do you hear? Seek!' Carrie hissed at him. He would chase off anywhere if you excited him, even if there was nothing there. He ran a few yards, bounced stiffly on the spot, looked back at Carrie.

'Seek!'

He barked sharply and ran off round the side of the house.

Priscilla watched him go without surprise or regret, as if she was used to being left behind.

'What did he hear?' the nurse asked uneasily.

'Diller's dogs,' Lester said.

'Do you really believe that story?'

'Everybody does.'

'I've not been long in these parts. I didn't know. Last night... Oh, my God, I wonder. I wonder if I heard...' She shut the book and got up. 'If it wasn't for that poor helpless child, I'd not stay another night under this roof. As it is, I'm going to phone my sister and get her over to stay the night with me. Mrs Agnew's veal and ham pie will do for the two of us. She left me enough for an army.'

She went along the path and up the step to the summer-house, where she bent over Priscilla and talked loudly.

'You stay there' (as if she could do anything else) 'and I'll be back in a jiffy.'

She went into the house and was out again quite soon. 'The phone's out of order,' she called from the terrace. 'Oh dear. Now I *know* I can't stay alone. Watch Priscilla a minute, there's good children, while I run down the road to the call box outside the Lord Nelson. Oh dear.'

Carrie went with her to the front of the house, because they were going to take Priscilla to the horses as soon as she was safely out of the gate.

When she was on the drive, there was an unearthly noise

55

of Charlie being chased by two or three dogs on the other side of the hedge. He was barking shrilly. They were baying after him in a pack.

'The dogs!' With a yelp of fear, the nurse jammed on her hat with one hand and scuttled out into the road, where she was hit by a car coming round the corner.

Ten

Carrie saw it and heard it. She shouted for Lester, and ran out to the road.

The nurse was lying in front of the car. Carrie didn't want to look. She had never seen a dead body.

The driver was out of the car and kneeling beside the nurse. She rolled over and said, 'Oh, my God,' so Carrie went closer and looked.

Her chill red face was redder still with grazes oozing blood. Her hat was off and her grey hair was lying about in wisps and strands. She lay on her back, staring at Carrie and the driver with one eye open and one swollen shut, murmuring, 'Oh, my God, my God, my God.'

'Are you all right?' The driver was a youngish man, with a dark suit and a row of pens in his breast pocket. 'Are you all right?' He bent his head and shouted, as if the accident had knocked the nurse silly, as perhaps it had.

'All right. Help me up.'

'You're not supposed to touch an injured person.' Carrie had been in the Guides for a term before they threw her out for having the wrong spirit. But he took hold of the nurse's arm and pulled her up to sit against the bumper of the car, rolling her eyes.

'What happened?' Lester ran out of the white gate and across the stream. He had grabbed a towel on the way, and he squatted and began to dab carefully at the nurse's poor grazed face.

The driver stood up. 'Fool woman.' Now that he saw she was all right, he was beginning to be quite cross which was not fair, since it was partly his fault for going too fast round a blind corner. 'She ran right out. Right in front of me.'

'She was frightened,' Lester said.

'What of?' the driver asked the nurse, but she shook her head. She could not remember. She closed her eyes and began to pass out, so Lester and Carrie and the driver got her up and into the front seat of the car.

'Who is she?'

'We don't know.'

'I'd better take her to the hospital,' the driver said.

'To the hospital ...' The nurse seemed to have forgotten about Priscilla.

'We'll send flowers.'

'You do that.' The driver got into the car and took the nurse away.

Lester and Carrie ran back to the house. If they had not run, if they had walked up the drive discussing whether it was their fault, Priscilla would have drowned, and perhaps Michael too.

As they came through the hall into the drawing-room, they heard him scream. The summerhouse step was empty. For a moment as they dashed out, they could not see Priscilla, and then they saw that she and Michael were in the swimming pool.

Priscilla was thrashing weakly with her arms, her white face appearing and disappearing in the churning water. Michael was going under, and coming up to scream and choke, and going under again in terror.

Lester seemed to jump right from the terrace into the pool. Carrie fell off the terrace, tumbled across the grass and dropped by the edge of the water, clutching for Michael's clothes. The back of his jacket floated up on an air bubble. She grabbed it and pulled. He was heavily water-logged. Somehow she managed to drag him to the side and get his hands on the rail. Frozen, they slipped off. She grabbed his wrists and hung on. His face was a bluish white. He stared at Carrie with eyes that had seen death.

Wriggling backwards, she managed to haul him up over the side, and he fell on to the grass, coughing and heaving up gallons of water.

Lester was still in the pool. He had one arm round Priscilla, and with the other hand was clinging to the wheelchair, which was bobbing upside down on the water.

'Help me!'

Under the diving board was a long pole with a net used for skimming leaves. Carrie thrust it out. Lester let go of the chair and grabbed it, and she was able to pull him to the side.

They got Priscilla out. Her long hair was streaked round her small peaked face. She was shaken with shivering and the chattering of her teeth, the skin shrunk away from her jaw like a skull.

'Your jacket.' Lester was shivering too, and gasping. He could hardly speak. He put Carrie's jacket round Priscilla and sat on the ground and hugged her, trying to get her warm. 'Get blankets.'

Michael was staggering on his feet now, still coughing, his hair and clothes soaked and clinging.

'Keep moving,' Carrie called to him. 'Run, jump.'

Michael tried to jump up and down in his squelching boots. He fell and began to cry. But Charlie had come back through the hedge. As Carrie ran into the house, she saw him leap at Michael and the little boy flung his arms round his thick coat and buried his head in the warm tangled hair and clung there, sobbing and shaking.

Carrie tore blankets off the beds in the first room upstairs, and wrapped them round Michael and Priscilla. Wearing his blanket like a Bedouin, Lester picked up the cocoon of Priscilla and carried her to the house. Carrie picked up Michael, but he was too heavy. He struggled and she put him down. He brought up a bit more water, then went with her into the house, trailing Mrs Agnew's pink blanket.

Carrie had to cut his red rubber boots off his wet feet.

'My boots!' Liza had bought them for him at the Jumble Sale.

Carrie hacked them off with a bread knife, and more water fell out of them on the kitchen floor.

Priscilla had not cried or made a sound the whole time. Lester had managed to pull off her fur boots, and she sat on the padded kitchen bench wrapped like a squaw, her wasted legs stuck out in front of her and her pale face solemn.

Tented in his blanket, Lester crouched in front of her and rubbed the narrow feet, which looked like pieces of white wood. Carrie rubbed Michael's feet fiercely with a towel, until colour began to come back into them.

'Are you all right?'

'I'm all right, Carrie,' he said hoarsely.

He got down from the chair and went to stand in front of Priscilla. The child looked at him, really looked for the first time. He grinned. She smiled.

'How did she fall into the pool?' Lester asked.

'The chair started rolling.'

'Did you move her off the step?'

Michael paused, then he gave a water hiccup. 'Yes. It got away from me.'

The kitchen was a comfortable warm room. Carrie opened tins of soup, and while it was heating, she went upstairs and found some things in Victor's room that Lester and Michael could wear, and dry clothes for Priscilla.

Victor's room had pictures of sports teams and bold prints of racing cars on the curtains and counterpane. On one wall hung an oar and a ski and an ice hockey stick and a squash racquet, all labelled with dates of famous victories.

Jane's room had more team pictures, and shelves of silver cups and trophies. Priscilla's room *was* in the turret. The round room was frilly pink and white, with juvenile pictures and cuddly dolls and animals, too young for her, as if she had not been given anything since the accident. By the curved window was a small chintz armchair with a footstool, where she could sit like a little old lady and look at the tops of the shrubbery trees and roofs of the houses in the village where the world began.

A pink and white prison, with frills and chintz and a rug woven with tumbling teddy bears. It was only as she went downstairs that Carrie remembered it was the spooky room, and wondered if she ought to have felt scared.

They changed their clothes in the kitchen, so as not to get another room wet. Carrie dressed Priscilla. It was a strange feeling, like dressing a big doll. She would let you do anything, but would not do anything for herself.

She sat at the table, with the bowl of soup steaming in front of her, and her hands in her lap.

'Eat your soup.'

She put on a spoiled whine. 'I don't want it.'

Opposite her, Michael picked up a spoonful of soup, opened his mouth like a cavern and plunged in the spoon, clacking it with his teeth.

'Yum, Bristler. Just what the doctor ordered for drownding.'

Priscilla stared at him, and presently the tip of her tongue came out and she licked her pale lips. Her hand crept out of her lap, picked up the spoon and dipped it into the soup. She began to eat, holding the spoon in her fist like a young child, staring at Michael.

She was a bit older than him, but she seemed much younger.

Eleven

When Carrie had moved the horses to fresh patches of grass, she went down the road to the telephone box outside the Lord Nelson.

There was no telephone at World's End, so she rang Mr Mismo.

'Who's that? What? What's up?' He always shouted into the telephone, as if it was an instrument used only for crisis.

'Could you please tell my mother that Michael and I are staying the night with friends? Say it's an emergency and they need us. She'll understand that.'

'No doubt she would, old chump, if she was there, but she's gone away with the Captain.' That was what he called Carrie's father. 'The Captain took a fit to go and look at his boat, and your Ma stopped by to tell the wife she wouldn't be going to the Bring and Buy Sale. Neither bring nor buy.'

'Will you tell Tom or Liza then?'

'I might.' Mr Mismo was eating. She could hear it through the telephone.

'I'm sorry if I got you up from lunch. But will you?'

'What makes you think they worry where you are?' Mr Mismo said triumphantly and rang off.

Carrie rang Lester's Mother, Mrs Figg, who was working today.

'Mount Pleasant, Matron speaking,' she began Mount Pleasantly, but when Carrie started to explain, she said, 'You tell that boy to get on home if he doesn't want a tanning.'

Carrie begged. 'Just one night. It's very important.'

From the other end of the line came the howl and thud and clatter of someone fighting on the stairs.

'All right, he can stay,' Mrs Figg said hurriedly. 'But I'll tan his hide when he does get back.'

She never laid a finger on Lester, nor did her mild husband, but she threatened him with fates.

'She'll tan your hide tomorrow,' Carrie reported to Lester. 'I hope it's worth it.'

'To spend the night at Brookside?' He grinned at her. It was an adventure. Most people only realize they have had an adventure after its over. With Lester, you were always aware of living an adventure while it was going on.

The sun was out all afternoon, so they put jerseys on Priscilla and three pairs of socks to fill up an oversize pair of boots which must be Jane's, and pushed her in a wheelbarrow to where the horses were grazing.

The wheelchair was still floating upside down in the pool like an abandoned paddle-wheel steamer.

'She hates it.' Michael spat into the blue water as they went by.

'It gets her about.'

'Pushed in front. I remember when I'd had that operation on my leg, I hated being pushed in front of people. Into a shop, everyone staring. Off the kerb into the traffic. If I had Bristler,' Michael said, 'I'd pull her behind me and let her see where's she's been.'

Lester pushed Priscilla up to each horse in turn, and she stroked them and smiled and seemed content.

'Want to ride?' Michael asked.

'No Mike, she can't,' Carrie said.

'Why not? She can sit, can't she? Want to ride Oliver Twist?'

'Yes.' Priscilla clenched her teeth. She gripped the sides of the wheelbarrow as if she could jump out.

Michael put the bridle on his pony and held him tightly while Lester and Carrie, standing on a bank, managed to lift Priscilla to sit in the saddle. She was afraid and excited at the same time, but as Michael led Oliver slowly forward down the grass track, with Carrie and Lester holding her knees on each side, the excitement was outweighing the fear. They had put her hands on the reins. Stiffly at first, but then she bent her fingers and flexed her wrists and lifted the reins to hold them in the right position. Her legs hung awkwardly, with the toes down. When they tried to put her feet in the stirrups, there was no strength in them, and they slipped out.

Her head usually sagged sadly on one side, as if life was not worth confronting. But now her head was up and straight. Her eyes looked at the place where the pony's

Priscilla gripped the sides of the wheelbarrow.

thick mane flopped between his ears. They took her round a muddy pond and through some pine trees to the edge of a slope, where she stared and stared at a pattern of fields and hedges and smoking cottage chimneys she had never seen before. As they turned and walked back towards the other horses, and Oliver whinnied as if he had been away for hours, something almost like a grin lifted her face.

But when Lester reached up to get her back into the wheelbarrow, the grin fell back to desolation and she put on that high baby wailing they had heard when her mother had snatched her away from the back gate.

'You can ride tomorrow.'

Priscilla wailed on. She was so babyish and spoiled. Somehow her mother had managed to give in to her, without actually giving her anything.

At the bottom of the garden was a building which had once been a stable. It now housed a lawnmower and roller and a clutter of toboggans, skis, skin-diving equipment, wheelbarrows, tools. They moved it all out and put the horses inside, Peter and John in one loose box and Oliver in a stall.

At dusk, Lester walked through the village to a house where there was a pony, and came back with a small sack of horse nuts on his back.

'How did you pay?' Carrie asked.

'My credit is good.'

'Did you steal it?'

'Would I?'

'Yes. No.' You never knew with Lester.

The Nurse was right when she said Mrs Agnew had left enough food for an army. They spent most of the evening eating. Priscilla stuffed veal and ham pie into her mouth and Charlie caught crumbs as they fell into her lap. Once, Michael thought she was going to laugh.

'Go on. Laugh. Charlie's funny.'

Michael laughed into her face, but she closed it and drew back.

'She's afraid.'

'What of?' Priscilla was withdrawn into her own world again.

'Does she hear something?'

Brookside was not a bit haunted during the day, but as night dropped quickly down, it was different. Turning on lights only made the outside world grow darker.

A dog barked, and Charlie sat up and growled.

Michael said, 'I want to go home.'

'Shut up.' Lester was listening.

'I want to go home,' Michael repeated, and fell asleep,

exhausted from drowning. Carrie pushed him up the stairs, grumbling and yawning, and put him into Victor's bed. He was too tired to realize he was not in his own room.

Lester wanted to sleep in the turret room.

'Rather you than me.' Carrie took Priscilla into the bed in Jane's room. It was an odd feeling to share a bed with someone who didn't kick and thresh about. When she had to share a bed with Em when they lived with Uncle Rudolf and Aunt Valentina, Em used to whirl like a top, drag off the blankets and kick Carrie on to the floor.

Priscilla lay so still that Carrie could not tell if she was asleep or awake.

'Are you asleep?'

'Yes,' Priscilla whispered with her eyes shut.

Carrie dozed, and woke in a panic. Where was she? Who was in the bed? She put out a hand and felt a soft wool nightgown. Priscilla had been lying on her back with her legs straight. Now she was on her side, with her legs drawn up as if, in sleep, some power came to them.

Carrie could not sleep. She turned on the bedside lamp by whose light Jane Agnew read *Your Advantage: How to Win at Tennis, and Judy Barnard, Olympic Medallist.* She listened to the night. Silence sang in her ears. In a shadowed corner, a tree seemed to grow up through the room. She thought of daft Diller crashing through the spinney behind the dogs.

She wanted to wake Lester, because he was not afraid. But it was because he was not afraid that she could not wake him, and admit that she was.

She thought of all the food that was still in the big refrigerator in the kitchen. She got up, called Charlie to go ahead of her, and went downstairs. A lamp was lit in the drawing-room. On the sofa, under the blind eyes of the flat-topped marble ladies, Lester was sleeping, rolled up in an eiderdown.

A board creaked under Carrie's bare foot, and he woke and sat up.

'What's the matter?'

'I'm hungry. You want something?'

'A piece of that treacle tart. With cream.'

'Did you come down because it was scary up there?'

'No. But the room's too girly. The bed's too short. Yes ... it was scary. There's a sort of – I don't know. Not a noise, but a feeling. I felt there were trees. I couldn't sleep.'

'How can Priscilla sleep alone there?'

'There's some people hear ghosts,' Lester quoted Miss Etty, 'and some that don't.'

Twelve

At breakfast on Sunday, Carrie said, 'Priscilla turned over in bed when she was asleep. Why does her mother say it's hopeless?'

'Her mother is a bag of old lard,' Michael said, just as Mrs Agnew walked into the kitchen.

She was too upset to hear. 'What's going on? What's Priskie doing?'

Priscilla was eating treacle tart with her fingers and wiping them on the front of a ribboned party dress she had wanted to wear. As soon as she saw her mother, she put on that high baby wail. Mrs Agnew lifted her out of the chair and held her, patting her back while the child wailed and dribbled treacle tart down her back.

'She can't digest pastry.'

'Last night she digested veal and ham pie.' The others had been put off their food, but Michael went on eating cake.

'What are you all doing here anyway? Where's Mrs Fassett?'

'In the hospital.'

'What happened to her? Oh, I knew it. I knew something

was wrong. You see, Brian.' Her husband had come into the kitchen in a sheepskin coat and Old Boys' muffler. 'When I tried to ring up yesterday and the phone was out of order, I was right to say we must come back early.'

'You were right, my dear' (as if he was used to that). 'Here, give me Priskie.' He put her down on the settee, where she sat like a dressed-up doll, her eyes gone blank. 'Where's her chair?'

'Outside,' Carrie said.

Mrs Agnew recognized her. 'You kids again! Why did Mrs Fassett let you in? What did you do to her? *What have you done with Mrs Fassett?*'

'She got run over?' Lester said it like a question, to make it sound not so bad.

'What by?'

'A car. She ran into the road.'

'Why?'

'She heard a ghost.'

'Oh rubbish, she's a fool.'

'It wasn't her fault. The car was going too fast round the corner.'

'I'll sue the driver.'

'He couldn't see round that high bank.'

'I'll sue the Rural District Council. They've been promising to level it ever since we came. I know you too.' She levelled her healthy blue eyes at Lester. 'You're the errand boy from the grocery.'

'Yes, Madam.' Lester did not bother to disillusion her. 'You're out of marge. May I deliver?'

'You may go. All of you. You've made enough trouble.'

She didn't know the half of it. They were not going to tell her about the drowning, but Mr Agnew called from the back door, 'What's the wheelchair doing in the swimming pool?'

'It fell in.'

'With Bristler in it,' Michael added honestly.

'Oh, my God.'

'Michael fell in too,' Carrie said.

'Was it his fault?'

His fault, his fault. Why did accidents always have to be someone's *fault*?

To rescue Michael, Lester said, 'He saved her life, as a matter of fact.'

Before Mrs Agnew could decide whether to be angry or grateful, Charlie came in from the back door, dripping wet from a morning's stroll through the undergrowth.

'Get that hideous brute out of here!' When she raised her voice, Priscilla began to wail again. 'Priskie's terrified of dogs.'

'She likes Charlie,' Michael said. 'She likes Oliver too.'

'Who's he?'

'Michael's pony,' Carrie said. 'Well, I mean, he doesn't *own* him. You can't own an animal, you see, any more than you can *own* a human being, since the days of slavery. An animal may live with you, but – well, it's like if you call a person "my friend", it doesn't mean you own them, because—'

Mr Agnew, coming in again from the back door, cut short her sermon.

'What are those horses doing in the shed?'

'Well, we were just going to tell you . . .'

'I won't have horses here,' Mrs Agnew said in horror. 'Priskie is terrified of horses.'

'She rode Oliver.'

'You're mad.'

'She liked it. It did her good.'

'Oh, rubbish,' Mrs Agnew said impatiently. 'It's no use.'

Priskie's given up, Victor had said. But it was the mother who had given up, not the child.

'It was an adventure,' Carrie said. 'She went down the track and saw the ducks in the pond and splashed through a puddle and went up the hill through those pine trees and saw that view on the other side. She couldn't go there in a wheelchair.'

'She won't go anywhere in that one,' Mr Agnew said. 'It's ruined.'

68

'I'll buy you another,' Michael offered, without hope.

'I ought to make you.'

'Brian.' His wife grabbed his arm. 'Priskie was in the pool. The little boy saved her life.'

'Did he, by Jove? Well now.' He rubbed his large chin, which was already beginning to bristle again after a morning shave. 'Well now. That was very fine.' He put his hand inside his coat and brought out his wallet.

'I don't want money,' Michael said, perhaps for the first time since they had come to live at World's End and never had enough. 'If you'll just let me come back sometime and play with Bristler.'

'You could knock me down.' Mr Agnew stared at Michael, then slowly put his wallet back in his pocket. 'You could knock me down with a shuttlecock. I never heard a small boy refuse money before. Good chap, good chap.' He slapped Michael so hard across the shoulders that he choked, and brought up the last drops of yesterday's swimming pool water. 'All right then, you may come and play with Priskie.'

'But don't bring that horse.' Mrs Agnew had to get in her two pennyworth.

Michael was just in time to get Miss Cordelia Chattaway to church. Carrie led Oliver home for him, and he puffed into Miss Chattaway's cottage and found her sitting ready in the old-fashioned Bath chair, with her velvet winter hat and her gloves and her little white boots side by side like sugar mice on the footrest.

'Good morrow, Sir Michael. Hast come to squire thy lady to the tourney?' She was a bit dotty, but she did love going to church.

So did Charlie. It was cool on the old stones in there for a dog who was always too hot indoors. He trotted by the chair into the village and down the lane where a straggle of cars and walkers were headed for the church, which was a hundred times too big for the number of people who went there.

So why shouldn't Charlie go in and sit with Miss Cordelia and Michael? He was shouldering in, with his shaggy hair bouncing, but the verger stopped him in the porch.

'Out,' he said.

'But, King—' Michael stopped the chair to argue in a whisper under the fine swelling surge of the organ.

'Yes, I know. King Charles carried his spaniel to church service, so ever since, they've been allowed in. My eyes may not be what they were, but that dog is not a King Charles Spaniel. Out.'

Charlie lay down to wait by the grave of Martin Arbuckle. Farmer of this Parish. *'As ye sow, so shall ye reap.'*

Michael pushed Miss Chattaway to the pew under the pulpit where she could nod and smile at the vicar, even though she couldn't hear the sermon. She rode happily up the aisle, nodding right and left to empty pews. She did not mind the chair. At the end of her life, she was glad of the rest. But Priscilla's life had not even properly begun.

Thirteen

When the horses were fed and turned out to join lonely braying Leonora, and Lester had gone home to get his hide tanned, Carrie went to the house.

She couldn't get in. The windows were shut. All the doors were locked. The ram and the goat were still in the shed, bumping their heads against the door. The chickens were still in the hen house, grumbling about late food service. Several dogs were inside the house, barking. Pip, the orange cat, was sitting in the side window with her tail curled round a flower pot and her whiskers spread against the glass.

'Where is everybody?' Carrie knew this window. Once when Lester had whistled under her bedroom to come down and watch rabbits dance on the moonlit hill, her father had locked up before she got back. From the tool shed, she got the old knife with which her mother pried out weeds round the front steps, and slipped the thin blade under the window catch. Pip moved just in time as the catch gave and the window swung inwards, knocking the flower pot on to the floor.

Carrie stood on the bottom of a bucket and heaved herself through the small window.

'Tom! Liza! Where is everybody?' They must be sleeping late. She let the dogs out, mopped up a puppy puddle, fed the hamster, gave milk to a nursing mother cat, and went upstairs.

Tom's room was empty, the bed unslept in. Liza's room was empty, the bed unmade, but then it always was. Her old dog Dusty, asleep on the rumpled blankets, lifted his moulting head to identify Carrie with a rheumy eye, then went to sleep again.

Carrie went down the passage and up the little crooked stairway to the small room which had once been a linen cupboard and was now Em's room. The door was shut. Carrie went in.

'I've told you not to come into my room without knocking.'

The middle shelf had been taken out, to make a bed with a mattress on the wide bottom shelf. In this boxed-in space, Em was sitting with a pile of papers on her knees. She jumped up and shoved the papers under the mattress, though Carrie was not remotely interested in them.

'Where is everybody?'

'Mum and Dad went to the coast. Liza went off yesterday and never came back. Tom went to look for her and never came back. Please get out of my room.' Em hated people in her room as much as a hibernating dormouse.

'Did Mr Mismo tell you where we were?'

'Sort of.'

71

'We stayed at Brookside to look after Priscilla. Were you alone all night?'

'Oh, I didn't mind,' Em said casually, although she had locked all the doors and windows and dragged a high-backed bench across the side door of what had been the 'Snug' behind the bar when World's End was an inn.

'Why didn't you feed the chickens, or Henry and Lucy, or poor Mother Hubbard, who's feeding seven, or—'

'Why do you always find fault?'

Tom came back late that evening with Alec Harvey, the vet. He had searched everywhere Liza might have gone, and had wandered half the day in the local town, since she had started life as a city girl. Finally he had gone to the housing estates at Newtown to see if Mr Harvey knew anything.

All Mr Harvey knew was that Liza had been getting more careless and clumsy, rude to touchy customers with pampered lapdogs, muddling telephone messages and even medicines, mixing up labels on the cat cages and the kennels, and finally starting a big shouting match with him, telling him he could keep his rotten job, and walking out.

'With my spare set of keys in her pocket. And I hate to say this, Tom,' he had admitted, 'but after she'd gone, I found I'd lost more than my keys.'

'Not money. Liza wouldn't take money.'

'How do you know? In the kind of life she's lived, brought up on the streets, having to fight for anything she got, if you see money, you take it. And disappear.'

'How much?'

'Twenty pounds. Mrs Cavendish had finally paid me. I knew it was too good to be true.'

At World's End, Alec told them about the shouting match, and how he had shouted back at Liza.

'A man can only take so much,' he said. 'That girl gets away with murder, because she's had rough luck and because I like her and I know she has the touch with animals, if she'll only let herself learn some techniques. When she yelled at me, "One day I'll walk out on you!", I told her to walk and keep on walking.'

'You can't say that to Liza,' Carrie said. 'She's had a hard life.'

'So have I.' Mr Harvey was tired and hungry. Em had given him some bread and milk, with brown sugar and the crusts on. 'I'm busier than ever with distemper and cat flu and road accidents and people going off skiing and leaving their dogs in the kennels. I don't know what I'll do if old Red doesn't come back.' He called Liza that, because of her hair and the bicycle she rode.

'She won't,' Tom said. 'For a while. Perhaps never.' Tom knew Liza better than anyone. He did not always understand her. But he knew. 'Look – I could help you out for a couple of weeks.'

'But Tom, you've got—' Em was going to say, 'You've got a holiday', but Tom shut her up with a look and went on, 'We're not so busy at the zoo. Jan could spare me.'

When Mother and Dad came back, Liza was still gone. Jerome Fielding was upset. Liza amused and attracted him. He liked having her about with her fiery swinging hair and temper, and the bold, comic way she did not care what she said to anyone. She had been helping him with the first chapters of *Sailor of the Seven Seas*, which were finished, more or less, with the author biting his nails down to the quick and swearing he would rather make a living pumping cesspools. He had won an old typewriter off a man in a darts game, and Liza, who had learned a bit at Mount Pleasant, had been typing out his unreadable handwriting.

'She's let me down.' He drew a mug of beer from the cask he kept behind the bar – the dogs licked up the drips from the spigot – and sat down to hunt and peck with two fingers on the stammering typewriter.

'She'll come back,' Mother said. She did not know about the money. No one did, except Tom.

'She won't.' Tom showed her a letter that had come with a far-off postmark, nowhere near where Liza had ever been.

'Got the jitters. Nothing to do with any of you. Got to get

73

off on my own and find out who I am.'

'She knows who she is,' Michael objected. 'She's Liza Jones. And she's a swine to leave Dusty.'

'She knows he's all right,' Tom said. 'She wants to be free and alone. Not depend on other people. Even a dog.'

'For ever?' Michael took the torn pamphlet, on the back of which Liza had scrawled her letter, and held it up to the light to detect invisible ink. 'GNIMRAF YROTCAF POTS,' he read, seeing the print of the pamphlet backwards.

'Not alone for ever,' Tom said. 'But you can only live with people if you've first found out how to live with yourself.'

'Have *you*?'

'Not yet. One day, I'll take off and find out who I am. So will you, Mike.'

'How will Bristler ever find out?' Michael wondered. 'She is a prisoner in that family.'

He had been over to Brookside, leaving Oliver tethered on a school friend's lawn, and walking the rest of the way.

It was not a success. Priscilla asked at once, 'Where's Oliver?' and then fell into blank disappointment.

Victor and Jane were at home, thundering through the house like Niagara. As they got noisier, Priscilla grew quieter. She wouldn't talk to Michael, or play the games he thought up. And when he went back for his pony, his friend had got on him and been bucked off on to his head, and Oliver had eaten all next year's hollyhocks.

So next time, Michael's father took him over in the groggy car, which sounded like a racer, even at fifteen miles an hour.

Mrs Agnew was charmed with Jerome. She had read of his sailing adventures in a yachting magazine. 'I like people who *do* things. I like people who get up and go instead of sitting at home talking about what they would do if they had the time. I'm going to cross the North Sea in a canoe, like the Norsemen, one day when I get time.' She was fighting with the Council about levelling the banked corner, trying to organize her village into a carol-singing parade, and trying to teach the local housewives to shop once a week instead of every day. People were beginning to wish she had never bought Brookside.

Dad was quite charmed with her too, because she had read about him, and seemed to know her stuff about boats. He promised to take her for a wild winter sail when the *Lady Alice* was out of the boatyard (good let-off for Mother), and Mrs Agnew was so delighted that she let him take Priscilla back to World's End.

The child had a folding canvas chair to take in cars. As soon as they got home, Michael wheeled her to the stable yard.

Oliver was too small to be able to look comfortably over his half door, so he was standing on his back legs, with his front feet hanging over the door like a dog. Michael pushed Priscilla near, and she put out a wondering hand and touched his hoof. Then she stroked the rounded fetlock with its soft winter plume, then felt the hard little hoof again. She seemed to be very interested in the feel of things. Oliver dropped his head and she put her fingers into his warm wet nostril, beaded with hairs like dew on mown grass.

'He'll nip.' Brought up a sailor, Michael's father was never at his ease with the horses.

'Not if you don't think he will,' Michael said.

'*Some put their trust in chariots,*' his father quoted, '*and some in horses.* That poor little kid is not afraid.'

'Of course not.' When his father had gone indoors, Michael asked Priscilla, 'You want to ride?'

'No, Mike,' Carrie called from John's loose box, where she was sitting in the manger. 'Her mother would be furious.'

'Her mother isn't here,' Michael said reasonably. 'You wait here, Bristler, while I get the tack.' Although it was silly to say 'Wait here' or 'Stay there' to her, somehow it seemed less insulting than just walking off and leaving her stuck. Mother felt that way about plants. 'You wait there,'

75

she'd say to an autumn crocus knocked sideways by a running dog, 'till I get something to prop you.'

When Michael had saddled Oliver and led him out, Carrie looked over John's door and said, 'You're mad. Like Mrs Agnew said.'

'Bristler loves it. Look at her face.'

'How do you know it won't hurt her?'

'Her legs are no good anyway,' Michael said, 'so what difference can it make?'

'You're ma-ahd,' Carrie said in Mrs Agnew's upper-class voice for lower-class people.

'Will you help me?'

'We mustn't go too far.' No need to say Yes. He'd known she would. 'Mr Harvey is coming to look at John's mane. I think he's got fungus.'

Fourteen

When the vet arrived on the marvellous big bay thoroughbred he exercised for a friend, Carrie and Michael had Priscilla on Oliver in the meadow.

It wasn't going well. The pony kept putting his head down to tear at grass, and pulling the reins through the child's weak fingers.

Priscilla was fine when things were easy. Any difficulty upset her, and she grizzled.

'For a great girl like you, you're an awful baby,' Michael said.

'Don't talk to her like that.'

'It's good for her. Get up, Ollie.' Michael slapped the pony in his fat ribs. He moved forward with his head down, and Priscilla squealed.

'Shut up, Bristler, and get your heels down.'

Your head and your heart keep up,
Your hands and your heels keep down.
Your knees keep close to your horse's side,
And your elbows close to your—

Get up, Oliver Twist.' Legs braced, Michael struggled to pull up the pony's stubborn head.

'You need a grass rein,' Alec Harvey called from the gate. 'Bring him in the yard.'

He took two lengths of baling twine and tied one end of each to the ring of Oliver's snaffle, above the reins. He passed the twine up through the loop of the browband and back to the D of the saddle. Oliver tried to get his head down to some spilled chicken feed, found he couldn't reach, and gnashed his teeth.

'Foiled!' Mr Harvey laughed up at Priscilla. He was a cheerful young man with honest eyes that showed you himself. Priscilla stared solemnly down at him, her hands clutching the brown and white mane.

'Is that hers?' He saw the wheelchair abandoned by the manure heap where Carrie and Michael had managed with difficulty and some danger to heave Priscilla on board.

'She can't use her own legs,' Michael said, 'so she uses Oliver's.' He grinned up at Priscilla, who gave him back her thin, uncertain smile, which did not quite reach her dark eyes. 'She likes to look down at people from a horse, instead of up from a chair.'

'Who gave you this idea?'

'She did. Why?' Was Mr Harvey also going to say, 'You're mad'?

'It's a good one. I've seen it do wonders for some handicapped kids I used to teach.'

'Teach Bristler.'

They went back into the meadow, and he showed Michael how to hold the leading rein behind the pony's chin and not walk in front of him, and showed Carrie how to walk alongside, holding the child's leg. Oliver moved steadily, flexing to the grass rein, his eye rolling back to check Priscilla.

77

'Is it sad to be a horse,' Michael asked him, 'and have to walk on your own food? It would be sad if we had to walk on bread and butter.'

They walked in a circle, and even jogged. A hint of pink showed in Priscilla's cheeks.

'Now she must do some exercises.'

'She won't.' Carrie remembered what Victor Agnew had said.

'Perhaps she will on a pony.'

Sitting on the bay thoroughbred, Alec Harvey showed Priscilla how to turn her body, raise her arms, touch her toes. But she stared at him and would not try.

'Come on, Bristler,' Michael urged anxiously. 'Do you good.'

'Try it,' Carrie said.

'I can't.'

'You can.'

Priscilla lifted her hands a few inches, then dropped them in a panic and wailed.

'Be a man, Bristler,' Michael said. 'It's to help you.'

'It's to help you ride the pony better,' Mr Harvey said. A fleck of spirit came back into the child's cautious eyes, and she tried feebly to copy the movements. Carrie kept one leg steady, but on the other side, her toes kept slipping down and back so that the stirrup knocked her ankle, and she cried.

'But it shows she's got some feeling there,' Mr Harvey said. He got off his horse to lift Priscilla down, and Carrie said at once, 'May I?'

'Five minutes.' He looked at his watch. 'I'm due at Crow Farm. Just one slow canter.'

Famous last words.

Carrie climbed up the side of the tall thoroughbred, put her feet into the leathers, and did four fast circuits of the meadow before she could pull up. Charging up the hill, along the short turf at the top, with the view going by like a train window, plunging down the hill, over the fallen tree, skidding round the duck pond, turning the horse just in

Carrie did four fast circuits of the meadow.

time before he jumped the fence, galloping over the flat bottom land where Mr Harvey shouted, 'Take it easy!'

'*If your horse won't stop with a strong pull,*' the books said, '*try a lighter one.*'

She tried. The books didn't always work. Finally a cat jumped out of a tree and the bay horse stopped dead and Carrie somersaulted on to her feet.

'Very neat,' Mr Harvey said, as he led back the horse,

who was not breathing as hard as she was. 'But take note, Priscilla. Not the correct way to dismount.'

Carrie went to tack up John to prove to herself that she really could ride with control. It was only when she was tidying his mane under the bridle that she realized that they had all been so interested in Priscilla, they had forgotten what Mr Harvey came for.

On Saturday, Mother cleaned the vet's house and surgery for him. She would not let him pay her. He was almost as poor as they were, because he would not send bills to people who had more animals than money. But he pushed a pound note secretly into her bag, where she found it later in the torn lining, couldn't imagine where it came from, and used it for his Christmas present.

Michael went with her to help.

'How's Priscilla?' Mr Harvey came in and found him kneeling on a chair before a sink full of soapsuds and test tubes and bowls.

'They won't let her come again. They found white hairs on her trousers and guessed she'd been on Oliver.'

'They're mad.' Good. So it was the Agnews who were mad, not the Fieldings. 'It could be a great chance for her. I'd love to go on with it. She might even get back some use of her legs, who knows? Stranger things have happened.'

'Stranger still if Mrs Agony let her,' Michael grumbled.

'Any good you asking them?'

'Perhaps if my father did ...' Michael made a diving bell with air in an upside-down beaker. 'She's in love with him.'

'Would he?' Mr Harvey reached over to tip the beaker and let the air bubble glop out.

'He might.' Michael glanced at his mother on top of a stepladder with a towel round her head, and whispered, 'He finds her very faccinating.'

'What did she say?'

When his father came back from Brookside, Michael was

80

waiting down the road in the rain with a sack over his head, jumping up and down to keep warm.

'She said No.' His father reached over to bang open the car door. One door would not open from the outside. One would not open from the inside. One would not open at all. The other would not stay shut.

'But then I gave her full helm,' he went on, as Michael slumped into the deflated seat cushion dejectedly, 'and she began to come up into the wind. When I told her Alec used to play County cricket—'

'He didn't.'

'He could have, if he'd had time. She did agree to let him talk to the child's doctor.'

'Oh – *luck*.' Michael bounced on the springless seat.

'Plus charm,' Jerome Fielding admitted. 'She wants me to go to her committee meeting about getting a sports field.'

'You go.'

'I don't want to, Mike,' he wailed, as if he was the son and Michael the father.

'You go,' said Michael sternly. 'It's in a good cause.'

The good cause got under way. They did not want Mrs Agnew to bring Priscilla to World's End, because she fussed and interfered and said that it was dangerous, and would do no good anyway. She protected the child too much, as if that could make up for her own guilt about the accident with the show pony. So Alec Harvey fetched her in his car twice a week, and with Michael leading and Carrie and Em on either side, Priscilla walked and jogged and learned to turn and stop the pony, and Oliver learned to stand as still as a Lifeguard's horse while she did the exercises. When it was too wet or cold for outdoors, they went round the earth floor of the big old barn, cleared of its centuries of dusty junk.

'Indoor equitation school. Very posh.' The cats sat in a row at the edge of the hayloft and stared down at the strange affair. 'Whoa there, lady.' Alec had a special jokey voice for the lessons. 'Bit wobbly today, aren't you? You seasick, Pris? You had a drop too much?' Smiling at the safe, feeble jokes, riding a pony like any other child, Priscilla began to work at strengthening her muscles, without knowing that it was work.

Fifteen

One morning before Christmas, everyone in the house woke to a strange light. Something had happened outside. There was a pale no-colour in the window, a flat white glare that led you in a leap from bed to the frost-flowered glass.

The world was full of snow.

The dogs plunged out, rolling in it, biting it, flinging white spray over their shoulders, haring off to pattern the trackless expanse of the meadow. Perpetua's last two puppies, Fanny and Jake, floundered behind, falling into drifts and coming up with white blobs for noses.

The cats didn't want to go out. In bad weather, they preferred the ashes in the fireplace. Last time Aunt Val and Uncle Rudolf, who actually owned this house, had come visiting after three days of rain, Aunt Val had said, when the fire was lit, 'What an extraordinary smell! Is it camphor wood?' To show she had been to Japan.

Em, who was tough with the cats because she understood them, pushed them all out and put a box against the flap in the back door so they couldn't come in. They stalked high-footed, very affronted, shaking their paws at each step. Some of them stayed on the doorstep, complaining that Em was cruel. Some went under bushes. Five-toed Caesar went into a tunnel in the woodpile where he was monitoring a squirrel burrow. Julius sat staring on top of the snow's crust, fluffed out, mortally offended at what had happened to his world overnight.

Oliver could sometimes open his stable door, if Michael forgot the bottom bolt. He had chosen last night to open it. When Carrie came to the gate, he was lying in the yard like a cake, mounded white.

'Why didn't you shelter, silly mountain pony? If you could get out, you could get back in.' She sat in the snow by his folded knees to play Which-hand-is-it with a lump of sugar. He was the only horse who would let you catch him lying down.

When she turned the others out, they raced off like mad broncos, bucking and kicking and tearing up at each other. John lay down to roll in the snow and Peter charged him. Peter pawed delicately, turned round and round with his tail lashing, sagged at the knees and flopped to roll, and John charged him. Oliver rolled when they weren't looking, and then all three charged off up the hill and stood at the top to stare into the dazzling view across the valley. Just as the donkey caught up, they turned and galloped down through flying white powder, skidded to a stop and began to paw away the snow to graze.

Michael came out to hang up a Miss Etty-type bird feeder on the oak tree. Em threw a snowball at him. Carrie jumped from the henhouse roof into a big drift, and they were all rolling in the glorious icy wet warmth. Blood sang. Cheeks caught fire. They were drunk on snow.

When Tom opened a window to call them for breakfast, Carrie threw a lump of snow straight into his face. He came out yelling, tripped over something buried, and fell with his long arms flung out, grabbing Carrie's scarf and dragging her down to wrestle in the way he used to do when he was half his height and Carrie was a baby.

He sat up suddenly, pushed Carrie away and shook snow from his wild hair like Charlie coming out of a pond.

'What's the matter, Tom?'

'I wish Liza was here.' He threw a lump of snow – splat! – at the goat shed door.

'Play with *me*!' Carrie pounced, but he pushed her off again and got up.

'I wish she was here too.' Carrie stumbled behind him up the invisible path. 'She'd love this snow. Won't she ever come back?'

'I think she'll stay away,' he muttered.

'Why? Has she done something?'

'Of course not. Shut up, kid.'

'Then why—?'

'You wouldn't understand.' Tom was grown up again. The yelling, wrestling boy was gone.

Breakfast was snow pancakes, Mother's invention, using two tablespoons of snow instead of each egg. It melted quickly in bubbles. The pancakes were thin and lacy. You rolled them round a blob of jam and ate as many as you liked, since snow was free.

Snow was delicious.

Too delicious to waste by staying indoors.

'Going to work, Jerry?' Mother asked.

'Work – with all that marvellous stuff outdoors? My dear woman, you must be mad.'

Lester came over with a tin tray and they all went up the hill with dustbin lids and the ancient sled that had been hanging in the barn when they first came here. The lids couldn't be steered, the tray spun round and spilled you off backwards. One runner came off the sled, and it tipped Carrie through the thin ice of the duckpond mud. She washed her face and hands with snow, and the sled settled quietly down on to the bottom ooze.

Michael had warped tennis racquets tied on his feet for snowshoes. He limped into the powdery snow instead of on top of it, disappearing up to his hood in a drift by the hedge. Tom had tried to make skis out of slats of wood, but they didn't work. Nothing worked.

At Brookside, Priscilla would be indoors looking out, while Victor and Jane would be skimming over the countryside on their painted skis. Mr Agnew would skate on the swimming pool. Mrs Agnew would drag her long red-cushioned toboggan up the hill above the village and rally the squealing children into an organized team.

But at World's End, nothing worked. Until Mr Mismo puffed across the fields like a snow plough, dragging the big wooden sled he had had as a boy. It was a monster heavy thing, with wooden runners, and ropes to steer it. There was room for Carrie, Lester, Em and Michael to cling behind Mr Mismo, who steered at the front, because it was his sled. Down the bare top slope, zigzag between two trees, putting on speed on the steep straight, quick swerve round the mound where a Roman soldier was supposed to be buried, Mr Mismo with a yell straightening out just in time to run head on into the snow buffer by the fence.

'Haven't had so much fun for years.'

His broad face was as red as one of his own fine tomatoes. His breath clouded the air. He shook Em and Carrie from on top of him and picked himself out of the snow and started up the hill again, pulling Michael on the sled.

'Come back, you old fool – you'll have a stroke!' Mrs Mismo had come to fetch him in the car. He pretended not to hear.

Later it grew grey and cold and the wind got up and blew blizzards off the trees. Tomorrow was Priscilla's day to ride, so Carrie and Lester and Michael warmed up by shovelling a path from the stable to the barn, and cleared off the milk churn platform which they used as a mounting block. It had a sloping ramp at one end, up which they could push the wheelchair, and Oliver had learned to stand very still while Priscilla slid over into the saddle.

Before they reached the barn, it was snowing again heavily, and blowing up for a big storm. The beginning of their path was already white again. After all the animals were fed and shut up, and Oliver bolted top and bottom, they went indoors.

Their mother had lit fires in all the fireplaces and heated bricks in the oven to warm everybody's bed. The storm rattled at windows, howled down chimneys and tore off some corner tiles with a clatter. It was going to be a rough night.

*

When everybody had gone up, Tom let the dogs out into the whirling snow. They all came in quickly, except slow old Dusty. He was used to bad weather, having been with Liza when she was living rough, on the road.

Was she on the road now? Her restless spirit could never settle long in one place. Calling to Dusty, Tom stared into the wild dark night, as if he might see Liza running down the vanished path with her long witch's cloak and her red hair streaming.

She would not come, of course. Because of the money. She had walked into World's End and out of it into another chunk of her life.

Upstairs, Tom heard the staircase window blow open. He went up to fix it, stuffing back the newspaper which kept out draughts. In the corner room, light showed under Carrie's door. She was sitting up in bed in three jerseys with her Horse Book propped against a dog. A puppy was keeping her feet warm.

'Can I see?'

She had been writing about Priscilla:

'If we who are free to run and jump find such great glory on a horse, what must it be for a prisoner in a chair?'

'Better blow out the candle,' Tom said, 'If you're going to get up early and shovel out the barn again.'

'Thank goodness for that barn,' Carrie said. 'Pris would die if she couldn't ride.'

In his parents' room, his father was lying with his beard outside the blankets, reading bits of *Sailor of the Seven Seas* aloud to Mother:

'I knew that something was amiss. When I raised the hatch, my horrified eyes were greeted by an appalling mess of oil and broken pipes...'

Mother was asleep.

So was Michael. Em was awake in her shelf bed, shuffling the piles of paper she had been working on for so long.

'Is that *Esmeralda's Book of Cats?*'

'No.'

'What is it then?' Tom thought she wanted him to ask.

'Not telling.'

'Don't then. Who cares?'

'Nobody.'

'They're all writing. Everybody in this house is writing a book,' Tom complained.

'Except you.'

'I could if I wanted to.'

'Do it then.'

'All right, I will.'

'See if I care.' You could never get the last word with Em.

In his room, Tom took the jacket paper off a book to write on the blank inside. Besides *Esmeralda's Book of Cats*, there was *Carrie's Horse Book* and *Michael's Book of Dog Lores*. This would be *Tom's Zoo Zayings*.

Anecdotes from his job:

'The skunk put its tail through the wire and it got bitten off by the kinkajou next door.

When we put broomsticks in the Squirrel Monkey cage for perches, they tore them out and beat each other over the head with them.

People say a zoo is good teaching for children. But all it teaches them is that it's OK to put animals in cages.'

Tom fell asleep.

In the middle of the night, he woke with a jump of his heart. He had never brought Dusty in!

He went downstairs and put on a coat and boots over his pyjamas. The wind was still blowing hard, rocking the old farmhouse like a boat at sea. The back door opened the wrong way, like most of the doors in this house. Tom could hardly push it out against the storm. Charlie slipped out with him and the door banged shut behind them, cutting off the light.

Calling and whistling uselessly into the wind, Tom struggled round the side of the house and climbed the gate into the yard, because the snow was too thick to push it open. Dusty might be sheltering under the grain shed, which was raised on big stones like toadstools. He had once gone in there when he was ill, and Liza had spent hours on her stomach trying to get him out.

'Seek, Charlie!'

Tom kicked away the snow in the gap between the shed and the ground, but Charlie would not look for Dusty. He was rushing in drunken circles, barking into the wind, jumping up at Tom as if they had fought their way out here for fun. The snow did not penetrate his heavy coat, but Tom was soaked and frozen. His hands and feet were numb. His face was so stiff that he could not whistle.

'Dusty!' Perhaps his lips would drop off. 'Dusty!' The cracked sound of his voice was thrown back at him with a faceful of snow.

The old dog could not live in this storm. 'I killed him,' Tom would have to tell Liza. If Liza ever came back.

Hopelessly he searched through the smothered yard among the strange thick shapes of familiar things blotted out with snow.

'Dustee-ee-ee!' His voice howled into the night. Charlie sent up a crescendo of hysterical barks as one end of the barn roof crashed in under a load of snow, the old thatch and timbers splintering in, snow falling steadily, stealthily through the gaping hole.

By morning, the sun was up and the sky a fierce bright blue over the sparkling white. Almost half the barn roof was gone. The edges of the lathing and beams hung inward as if they had followed the drop of a bomb.

Mr Mismo said, 'Might as well pull that whole great old ruin down as waste money to fix it.'

But Michael set his jaw. 'We'll fix it.'

Tom came down from the ladder where he had been looking at the damage.

'Pretty hopeless, Mike.'

'Don't *say* that to him,' Carrie raged.

'Sorry. Poor Mike.'

'Poor Bristler. She won't be able to ride.' Michael pulled

his hood down over his eyes and plodded through the snow to tell Oliver.

Harry, yellow son of Perpetua and Charlie, who was a throwback to some famous hunting dog, was tracking something over the snow, tail doing double time. They followed him as he whined, and pushed between a wheelbarrow and a roller in the cart shed. At the far end, behind some trunks and under part of a rusted plough, Dusty was lying like an empty sack. Clouded eyes, all his limp bones showing, too ill even to shiver, he was just alive. Only just.

Sixteen

The vet gave the old dog an injection, and he rallied a little, but was still very ill with pneumonia. He lay on Tom's bed and could only move his tail feebly when anyone came in with warm milk or broth, or just a pat and a comforting word. Alec Harvey said his chances were about forty-sixty.

'Sixty he lives?' Carrie asked.

Alec shook his head. 'The other way round, I'm afraid.'

'If he could just live till Christmas . . .'

'Why that day?'

'I think Liza might come back for Christmas.'

'Forty-sixty chance?' Alec smiled.

'Sixty she *will*.'

Some people think that if you want a thing to happen, you have to keep saying it won't. Carrie believed that you had to keep saying it would.

The barn roof was going to cost an enormous amount of money to repair. A local man would do it, but only with a down payment in advance.

'Don't you trust us?' Dad protested. 'We've got the money.'

'If so, it won't hurt to pay a bit of it then, will it?'

They did not like the man, or his style of reasoning, but he was the only builder who would tackle the old structure, and thatch it as well. Somehow, the money must be found.

The soup can bird feeders were going fairly well, selling door-to-door, but soon they had exhausted all the local doors. It took time to range farther afield, and was even more discouraging to have doors slammed in your face after you had trekked down a long muddy lane to a lonely farm.

'Feed the birds?' The farmer said to Em in disgust. 'I try to keep the wretched things away from my winter cabbages, not invite them.'

He banged the door. Em made her prehistoric ape face at it and trudged back down the lane.

Spider Monkey was in use again – Mother was using it to get to a holiday job at a hotel – but only half paid for. Every time Em went past Dick Peasly's garage, he looked at her sadly through the window of his repair shop, as if she was depriving his small children of their Christmas presents. Em had to make detours to get into the village another way.

Christmas was going to be a problem anyway. There would be no money for presents this year. Because they needed the barn for Priscilla's riding lessons, everything had to go into the red flour crock in the larder, labelled 'Raising the Roof'.

'Why the larder?' Mr Mismo asked when he came to put in his contribution, a five pound note and an old War Bond Certificate dating from no one knew which war. 'Burglars always want food.'

'Then they wouldn't come here.' Mother laughed, but she tied a string round the neck of the flour crock and hung it from the hook in the kitchen rafter, where hams and pheasants and sides of bacon used to hang in the old days. The crock hung over the heads of the family at the round table, reminding them of Priscilla.

Once, tilting his chair back after a meal and blinking

through the smoke of his pipe at the hanging crock, Dad said, 'Why don't we touch the Agnews for a little cash? It's their child, after all.'

Everyone said, 'No!' without even considering it.

'They only let her come here,' Em said, 'because it gets her out of their hair twice a week.'

'I thought it was because I charmed the mother.' Her father let down his chair. 'If not, why am I going to her blasted committee meetings?'

'They don't really want her to ride,' Carrie said. 'They think it's dangerous. They think it's no use.'

'They think Bristler is a lost cause,' Michael said.

'If she can't be perfect, like the others,' Lester said, 'she'd better be shut away. Helpless.'

'Don't be bitter, young Figg,' Dad said, but Mother said, 'Lester could be right. That's why Priscilla wouldn't make any effort with exercises, at the hospital.'

'She knew Mrs Agony had given up.' Michael was gouging deep into the initials P.A. that Priscilla had scratched on the round table last time she was here. 'Well, *we haven't.*' The penknife slipped on a knot and nicked his finger. He rubbed the blood into the A. 'Sweared in blood, Bristler. I won't give up.'

Lester and Carrie looked at each other, remembering the time when they had sworn in blood to save John from the slaughterhouse. They had banged the backs of their hands with a hairbrush, whirled their arms to make the blood start, and pressed the back of their hands together. Exchanging a message, as they were able to, without words, they both got up and went outside.

They had long had a dream of buying the pasture across the lane for hay and extra grazing. They would pull out the ragged hedge to make it part of World's End, and put gates across the lane, so that people coming this way would have to pay toll to get through.

They couldn't buy the field, and they couldn't shut off the lane – but they took John and Peter, and Michael's toy pistols and an empty tin can, and waited on the horses at either side of the lane. Carrie was wearing a black stocking over her head with holes for eyes, nose and mouth. Lester was wearing the big bush hat Jerome Fielding had brought back from Australia, turned up on one side with the brim pulled over his face.

When a car or a van or a motorbike or a bicycle came by, they pushed the horses out to block the road, pointed the pistols and yelled, 'Your money or your life!'

The first thing that came was the Post Office van.

The first thing that came was the Post Office van.

'Thanks for stopping.' Carrie lowered the gun and her highwayman voice. She had been afraid no one would stop.

'Got a parcel for you.' The postman handed her up a box. It was a Christmas present from the fat little nurse with the pearl barley teeth who had looked after Mother when she was hurt in the fire. He drove on before they could get back to the subject of money.

The next three cars gave them something. One willingly. One grumbling. One saying, 'I think it's wonderful what you children do. Is it for the Cruelty to Animals?'

'Yes,' Carrie said, and held out the soup tin. And afterwards, though she did not need to justify it to Lester, 'Well, Priscilla is a small animal, isn't she?'

They waited in the lane all afternoon. The horses got cold and restless, and Carrie and Lester got cold and bored. Very little traffic came by. Some of it did not even stop, but drove on through, hooting them out of the way. A bicycle yielded a few pennies. Grandad Barker on his old-fashioned tricycle that was said to have fought at the Battle of Hastings, dismounted creaking and groaning, took off two layers of clothes, searched through the rest for a pocket, turned it inside out to show it was empty, and climbed back into the outer layers and on to the trembling tricycle. Meanwhile a sports car and a plumbing van had got by, and Mrs Potter from Orchards, who shouted 'Is it an accident?' and drove quickly on in case it was.

They had made about thirty pence.

'Let's come out early tomorrow,' Lester said, 'and get people on the way to work.'

Before they went in, they stopped a yellow cement mixer truck going home. The driver stopped his rotating drum behind the cab to hear what they were saying.

'Money or your life!'

'What's that? What's that about my wife?'

Carrie pushed John nearer, though he did not like the truck. 'It's for the handicapped—' she began, but the man said, 'We gave to that last week,' and threw the mixing drum into gear with a rattle and a crunch. John leaped backwards into the dry ditch between the lawn and the road. Carrie fell off. The man said, 'Kids!' and drove on.

John went off towards the stable. Carrie lay on the cold hard ground, waiting for her head to clear.

'Let's not come out tomorrow,' she said.

Her father knew where the money must come from to save the barn for Priscilla.

He shut himself into the front parlour with the foot-stool against the door and wrote steadily for three days and most of three nights. He staggered out with his manuscript, croaking, 'I've finished it. It's finished me. But I've finished it. *Daily Amazer*, here it comes.'

'Will they pay you?' Michael asked anxiously.

'As soon as they see it. Let's go down to the Post Office and give Bessie Munce the thrill of stamping the Best Seller of the Age.'

Bessie Munce was not in the least thrilled. She weighed the package as if it were no more than a bundle of shoes left behind by somebody's visiting niece.

'That's a heavy parcel.' She looked over her spectacles through the fireguard on the counter that protected her from bandits. 'Cost you quite a bit, that will.' She sucked in what would have been her teeth if she had had them in. She always behaved as if Parcel Post was reckless extravagance.

'It can go book rate,' Michael's father said proudly.

'Printed matter?' Bessie asked sharply.

'It's typed. It's my book. I wrote it.' He could not resist raising his voice. There were two people in the other part of the shop which sold sweets and cigarettes and newspapers. They did not look round. Bessie Munce did not look up. She stamped the package, gave the change and threw *Sailor of the Seven Seas* over her shoulder into the canvas mail-bag.

Seventeen

Uncle Rudolf and Aunt Valentina had sent down a huge turkey – with instructions how to cook it, which didn't please Mother, and a note to say they would come and help eat it, which didn't please anybody.

'Unless,' Dad said, 'we could get Rudolf to help pay for the barn ... Who'll ask him?'

'You.'

'He doesn't like me.'

'He's your brother.'

'That's why.'

'Will Tom hate me when he's old and bald like Uncle Rhubarb?' Michael asked.

'Probably,' Tom said. 'I'm going to give my presents early tomorrow before they come. They won't approve of any of them.'

Tom gave animals to everybody.

A kitten for Mother. 'Just what I need!' Two cats jumped off her lap as she got up to see the white half-Persian in the basket.

An Ant Farm for his father, which Tom had made from the glass tank whose goldfish had kicked the bucket long ago, in spite of Mr Mismo's brandy administered with an eye-dropper. Tom had replaced the ends of the tank with strips of wood, so that the glass sides were quite close together. Filled with sand, you could see the ants' tunnels and burrows and underground store rooms.

Dad put it on the dresser, and one of the cats, leaping away from the new kitten, which had mobilized itself into a puffball of aggressive white fur, knocked the Ant Farm over.

Earthquake in the ant world. But ants are used to the natural calamities of feet and spades and broom-happy housewives. Patiently, they started to tunnel and build all over again.

Someone gave Michael a ball. He threw it for Jake, and knocked the Ant Farm over again.

'My deep personal sympathy in your disaster.' Lester, who might have been some kind of insect in an earlier life, put the glass tank on a high shelf of the dresser, where the black ants sorted themselves out of the chaos and got to work once more. 'The very best of luck.'

Tom gave Em a guinea pig which Jan Lynch had given him. He had been keeping it in his room with poor ailing Dusty while he was on holiday from the zoo. It had a face like the man at the grocery: the forehead, nose and chin all in one stodgy line. So Em called it Treacle, because the grocer was always trying to sell you big cans of treacle he had bought too much of.

When she picked him up, he clung sleepily, nosing her chin and quivering.

'He loves me.' She looked over the top of his sandy grocer's head.

'He has to,' Tom said. 'Guinea pigs can't hate because they don't have anything to fight with. That's why they wake when it's dark, so they can run away.'

Charlie, who loved small animals, and would follow a terrified fieldmouse with his nose down right across the yard, was very much moved by Treacle. He stood over his box, wagging his tail and whining. When no one was looking, he picked him out and carried him round for a while. Em put him back, but Charlie took him out again. Poor Treacle's fate was to be always soaking wet.

Tom gave Michael a Dutch rabbit, white in front and grey behind, divided evenly round the middle. It was a male, but Michael called it Phillis, because he wanted it to have babies.

For Carrie, a puppy which someone had dumped on Alec Harvey. A car had come into the vet's drive, a door opened, an arm threw the pup out sprawling on to the gravel, the door slammed and the car drove off before Alec could run out.

It was some kind of spaniel, brown and white and silky, with elephant ears and enormous feet. His name was Dump. He had come to the right place. World's End was a dumping ground for unwanted animals.

When Carrie put him down to meet the others, Perpetua sighed and got up – one more, was there no end to it? – and began to lick him expertly.

Tom gave Lester a cage of Peking robins which he had seen in a shop in the town, with a holly-decorated sign, 'GIVE A YULETIDE REDBREAST.'

Caught wild, the birds had been flown from China in

their thousands, crammed into tiny cages, shoulder to shoulder on the perch.

'GIVE A YULETIDE REDBREAST. THE SPIRIT OF CHRISTMAS.'

Tortured birds – to celebrate the birthday of Christ?

Everybody went outside and watched while Lester took the cage to the edge of the beech wood and opened the door. One by one, the frightened birds hopped into the doorway, stretched their cramped wings, looked round to make sure they were not being tricked once more, and flew off into the trees.

'Will they be all right?' Carrie asked. 'Mightn't they die?'

'A few,' Lester said. 'But they'll die free.'

Tom also had a present for Liza. He had bought it before she ran off, a tartan collar for Dusty. Now Liza was gone and Dusty might die. He had lived to see Christmas, but he was still very weak. Tom's room was too cold, so he lay wrapped in a rug in the warm corner behind the stove. They fed him warm milk and sugar and water from a spoon. His breathing was difficult and his body sank in as the life slowly left it.

Bending over him to try and make him look at the tartan collar, Michael said, 'I think he's dying.'

'Then don't watch him,' Tom said. 'Dying is private. You do it alone.'

Michael hung the collar on the Christmas tree. Even if Liza did come home today, she might be too late for Dusty.

Carrie and Em and Michael had made a present for Priscilla. It was a little dolls' schoolroom, because she couldn't go to school, fitted into three sides of a wooden box. It had matchbox desks, a blackboard and sliver of chalk, toothpick pens which dipped into a thimble of real ink, maps rolled round a pencil, tiny pictures made from stamps, a teacher doll with a bit of Carrie's hair wound round her head, pupils dressed by Em in scraps of her old gym tunic.

Their father drove them over with it to Brookside. Lester went home, because his mother had threatened him with the business end of the drumstick over his ear if he was late for turkey dinner. Also he did not like Victor Agnew.

They found the family in the drawing-room in a sea of wrapping paper and ribbon. The sofa where Lester and Carrie had eaten treacle tart in the middle of the night and listened for old Diller and the baby was covered with books and games and new clothes. The marble ladies under the mantelpiece wore necklaces of holly, but looked no jollier. In the French window was a huge tree hung with costly shining ornaments, and lights that flashed on and off in changing colours.

The tree at World's End was a small scrub pine dug out of the back of the hill, and decorated with strings of popcorn and nuts, painted fir cones, and real candles fixed on with clothes pegs.

Victor took Carrie outside in the snow to watch him hit the new tennis trainer game with his new aluminium racquet.

'I'm cold,' she said after admiring him for a while. 'Have a go then.'

She swiped and swatted, but she could not even get near the swinging ball.

Victor took back the racquet. 'You've got no eye.'

Carrie went into the house.

While the grown ups had eggnog with rum and nutmeg, Jane made Em play a game with dice. Em did not much like dice games, or any other kind, because it made her sulk if she lost. She lost. She sulked. Jane said she was a bad sport. In this house, that was like saying you were a murderer.

Neither Victor nor Jane had looked at the doll's schoolroom since Michael carried it in with his stomach and tongue stuck out, but Priscilla was delighted. She sat smiling by the table, and Michael pointed out to her its charms, like a house agent.

'She is better, isn't she?' Mother was drinking eggnog with Mrs Agnew while the men talked sailing in special gruff voices.

98

'She's all right.' Sometimes she talked as if there was nothing wrong, sometimes as if it was hopeless. Which did she really believe?

'The riding is doing her so much good.'

'I don't see any difference,' Mrs Agnew said in her clear, carrying voice. 'She can't ride anyway, with the barn gone.'

Michael looked round at her small note of triumph. She did not want anyone else to help Priscilla.

'I always thought it was too dangerous anyway,' she said. 'Quite mad.'

Eighteen

'I am going mad.' Aunt Valentina fell into a chair, shot up as a cat yowled and escaped, sank down again with her doeskin boots stuck out. 'It's too much. I am going mad.'

Poor Val. She did have bad luck. When she and Rudolf came to World's End, which was only just often enough to remind everybody whose house it was, she was either chased by the ram, butted by the goat, tipped off the donkey, or had her foot trodden on by a horse. Today when she arrived loaded with Christmas spirit and parcels, with miniature gold angels dangling from her ears, she ran full tilt into Tom carrying a dead dog, Carrie and Em and Michael behind him with candles, chanting.

Val's Christmas spirit left her in a flash. 'I am going mad.'

The procession went on out of the side door to the place under the weeping willow where dead animals rested, and where Michael had asked to be buried, 'when my time comes'. He had already made his own gravestone, the blade of a broken oar stuck into the ground and painted with the message, *'Micel Fidling. At Rest With His Friends'*.

At Dusty's graveside, Carrie recited a short poem she had quickly run up when he died at noon:

> *'Here the good old friend of Liza Jones,*
> *A wanderer dog lays down his weary bones.*
> *He mustn't be forgotten, must he?*
> *For all his name, he was not so dusty.'*

When they went back in, Valentina had recovered from the shock of having a dead body carried out as she came in, but she started up again when Dad lit the candles on the tree. The other lights were out, and it looked heavenly, the small pure flames like stars.

But Val screamed, 'Fire! It will catch fire!'

She lunged forward to blow out the candles, and knocked one off the tree. It set light to a piece of tissue paper on the floor.

'Leave it alone, Val.' Jerome Fielding put out the small fire with his foot. 'We'll blow them out when they get lower.'

'Go ahead, Jerry.' Uncle Rudolf was genial enough to-day, though his marble head and stiff back were not made for it. 'The insurance money is worth more to me than the house.'

Aunt Valentina, who hid a kindish heart under stupidity and narrow ideas, had brought presents for everyone.

For Mother, a small gold box. 'Because you like unusual jewellery, having been on the stage.'

'She doesn't wear—' Em began, but her mother shrieked as she opened the box.

'It's alive! Oh, my God, Val, it's alive.'

'Well, you like pets, don't you?'

'Yes, but – oh, my *God*.'

It was a beetle, about an inch long, with tiny coloured jewels stuck all over it. Round the edge of its body was a thin gold chain ending in a gold pin, to be fastened to—

'You – you wear it?' Mother put a hand on her blouse as if she could feel it there.

'Of course. It comes from South America. Living Brooch, they call it. It was very expensive.'

'Generous of you, but—'

'Don't you like it?'

'I hate it,' Mother said in a small voice. She tucked back her hair behind her ears and looked as if she were going to cry.

'I'd wear it,' Valentina said. 'I once had earrings which were two little globes of water with tiny fish in them. I'm fond of Nature, you see.'

Tom was trying to get the gold chain off, but it was embedded.

'What can we do with it?' Mother could hardly bear to look at the martyred beetle. 'We can't turn it loose looking like that.'

'I'll take it to the zoo,' Tom said.

'When is that boy going to get his hair cut?' Val wanted to know.

After dinner, they sat round a big fire in the front room. Uncle Rudolf and Dad sang a brothers' duet, in different keys. Michael sang in a tuneless drone, gasping for breath in the middle of words. Tom did three conjuring tricks and forgot how to finish the third.

'Then I'll have my money back,' Valentina said. 'When is that boy going to get his hair cut?'

Nobody wanted Em to sing, but she was persuaded to recite some of the angel's part she had rehearsed for the school play.

'... *Now while the white Frost King rides through the night,*
With eyes of ice and hoary eyebrows white ...'

Someone laughed and Em stopped and sat down.

When it was the first night of her own play, *Life and Death of a Star*, when the whole theatre rose and shouted, 'Author! Author!' and she came on stage in a shimmering gown with an armful of roses as long as a baby ... then, no one would laugh.

When it was her turn, Carrie launched into Masefield's 'Right Royal':

> '*An hour before the race they talked together,*
> *A pair of lovers in the mild March weather,*
> *Charles Cothill and the golden lady, Em.*'

'My sister?' Michael interrupted.
'Shut up.'

> '*Beautiful England's hands had fashioned them.*
> *He was from Sleins, that manor up the Lithe,*
> *Riding the Downs had made his body blithe* ...'

It went on for ever.

'Does she know the whole thing?' Uncle Rudolf asked nervously.

'I can do you the whole of *Reynard the Fox* too, if you like,' Carrie said.

> '*Right Royal was a bad horse in the past,*
> *A rogue, a cur, but he is cured at last* ...'

Uncle Rudolf dropped lightly off to sleep.

Carrie's voice gave out before the end of the poem. He woke, rather cross, belched, and said, 'Time to go, Val.'

Now or never about the barn.

'Before you go.' His brother Jerome cleared his throat. 'There's – er, just one – er, thing.' He was always lending money and never getting it back. He hated being the one who asked. 'I hate to tell you, but we had a bit of bad luck in the storm.'

'Don't tell me,' Rudolf said frostily. 'I saw it as we were driving in. "Look what they've done to my fine barn," I said.'

'And I said, "Don't be angry at Christmas, Rudie,"' his wife put in.

It did not sound likely, either for Val to say that, or for Uncle Rudolf to worry about a damaged barn, since the whole place had been a shambles before the Fieldings rebuilt it with love and labour.

'We've found a man who can repair it,' Mother said.

'Waste of money. I'd rather tear it down and build a modern bungalow to sell at profit.'

It was not for nothing that Rudolf was known as 'The Prince of Plumbers'. His plumbing business had grown to princely size by just such ruthless methods.

'We'll get the barn fixed,' his brother said stubbornly.

'Not worth it. You don't need it.'

'We do, Uncle Rhubarb.' Michael looked up at him, his tired eyes ringed with dark shadows. 'We've got this friend, you see. She's hankidapped. Like me.' He raised his short leg. 'She can't walk, so Oliver and I are teaching her to ride.'

'Who's Oliver?'

'My pony.'

'It sounds insane. If she can't walk, she certainly can't ride a horse.'

'She can, Uncle Rhubarb.'

'Don't call me that.'

'But it's too cold outdoors. We must get the barn mended.'

'Who's paying?' Not Rudolf, that was clear.

Michael was silent. A tear ran down his nose and he licked it into his mouth.

'I'm paying.' His father stood up.

'Ha! What with?'

Christmas, like too many family Christmases that start out quite promising, was ending in a quarrel.

'I finished my book, I told you.'

'Your book.' Rudolf pulled down his long top lip scornfully. 'You'll be lucky if you ever get a penny out of that.'

'It's going to be published.'

'That'll be the day.'

They faced each other, as they must have faced each

other long, long ago, when they were fighting small boys.

'The newspaper will print it.'

'You say so.'

'They say so. They've accepted it. They love it.' In des-

Dad embroidered the lie. 'They've accepted it and they love it.'

peration, Dad had to embroider the lie. 'So how do you like that?'

'I like it very much,' his brother said with a chill smile. 'Very much indeed. I've been thinking for some time – I didn't want to press you, but now that your book is such a success – I really ought to ask you to pay some rent for World's End.'

Nineteen

With that disaster, Christmas sputtered out like a spent match. It was given its death blow when Liza's mother arrived on Boxing Day in her vulgar purple van with 'E. ZLOTKIN, GREENGROCER. YOU WANT THE BEST? WE HAVE IT' painted on the side. She had gone back to her maiden name of Zlotkin when Liza's father left her.

She had been in some boozers on the way and was noisier and shinier than ever, and a bit matier than usual.

'Me and little Hubert just stopped by to bring you the compliments of the season.'

She opened the back of the van and dragged out a blubbery boy, half asleep. 'Remember dear little Hubert?'

Hube the Boob. How could they ever forget? Last summer, Mrs Zlotkin had only let Liza stay at World's End if Hubert came for the holidays.

'Same old boring old stinking dump.' His piggy eyes surveyed the kitchen for food.

'We've got some more puppies and kittens.' Carrie made a feeble attempt to be nice.

'Same old stinking menagerie.'

'I can smell that old dog of Liza's.' Mrs Zlotkin sniffed with her fat beery nose.

'You can't,' Carrie said. 'He died.'

'None too soon. She upset?'

'She doesn't—' Carrie began, and Tom put in quickly, 'She's gone away for a bit.'

'Where to?'

'A friend. In Liverpool.' All the family had this habit of spoiling a good lie by embroidering it.

'Funny.' Mrs Zlotkin let down her weight on a chair,

105

kicked off her shoes and picked her teeth with a match. 'The postmark wasn't from there.'

'You've heard from her?'

'Could have knocked me down. She never writes.'

'What did she say?' Tom tried to sound casual.

'I dunno. Can't read her writing. She sent me a present.'

'Money.' Hubert smacked his lips. Money and food were his Things.

'That's right. That's why I came. To thank her. Me thank Liza! Never thought I'd live to see the day. I'd – well, I'd got behind with the rent of the shop, see. I wrote Liza I was worried they'd turn me out. Not that she'd care. I never expected no answer. Certainly not twenty pounds.'

'Twenty pounds!' Carrie gasped. 'Where did she get that?'

'Nicked it, I daresay. Like she used to do when she was short of cash.'

'Not Liza?' Carrie looked at Tom, but he didn't say anything.

'Why not? For her poor old Mum. I always said she was a good girl.'

'You said she was bad,' Hubert said. 'And she is.'

There was an apple on the dresser shelf. He stood on a stool to reach it, lost his balance, clutched at the shelf and knocked the Ant Farm to the floor.

It did not break, but all the tunnels were blitzed, and black ants were coming out of the open top. Hubert screamed, tore at his clothes and rolled on the sofa as if in a fit.

'They're on me! I'm crawling!'

Hube the Boob. He was so awful, it was a gift.

When Alec Harvey arrived to eat cold turkey, he saw the purple van and hid in a cupboard till Mrs Zlotkin had gone.

'Dreadful old bag.' He came out picking a spider off his hair. 'Old Red Hates her.'

'She sent her twenty pounds,' Carrie said, 'to pay the

rent.' She saw Alec and Tom glance at each other. 'What do you know that I don't know?'

'Nothing. I wish we did,' Alec sighed. 'If Red doesn't turn up before Tom goes back to the zoo, I'll have to find someone else for her job.'

'Find me,' Carrie said.

'You have to go to school.'

'Who made that lousy law? They ought to be shot. I want a job. We need the money.'

Outside the window, they could see the snow coming down again, big soft flakes mounding the mounded bushes.

'Poor Bristler.' Michael held Phillis up to twitch his nose at the cold window pane. 'Will it never be spring?'

Tom went back to stay the night with Alec Harvey. They were operating first thing tomorrow, and there was no early bus.

As he turned into his street in the Housing Estates, Alec said, 'Funny. I don't remember leaving lights on.' The waiting-room and surgery windows were bright. 'Must be getting senile.' When he put his key into the side door, it wasn't locked. 'I need a keeper.' He opened the door.

On a waiting-room chair, a man was sitting with his hands on his knees, staring at the opposite wall.

'Hello?' he said. 'Who's that?' He was blind.

'I'm the vet,' Alec said. 'I thought I locked up.'

'She brought me in.' The blind man tilted his head towards the door of the surgery without looking at it.

'She—?' In two strides, Tom was across the room and through the door. Liza turned round, shaking back her hair. Her hands in rubber gloves were busy with a large yellow labrador lying limp on the operating table.

'Just in time,' she said. 'I've clamped the artery, but I can't get the ligature under. I'm afraid she'll move. Hold her, Tom.'

Without asking questions, he put his hands firmly on the labrador.

'What's going on?' Alec came in.

107

'Cut artery. But she's restless. I'm afraid she'll move before I—'

'What did you give her?'

'Tranquillizer into the muscle. I didn't dare give anaesthetic by myself. She's lost too much blood anyway. I injected 1 cc of Novocaine round the wound.'

'Not quite enough. She's feeling it.' When Alec had injected some more Novocaine, he scrubbed his hands quickly, put on rubber gloves and tied off the cut ends of the artery in the dog's front leg. Liza released the clamps after the knots were tied, and handed Alec the curved needle and suture she had prepared for closing the wound.

None of them talked until the stitching was done and the leg tightly bandaged, and the blind man brought in from the waiting room to lay his hand on the labrador's sleepy head. Her tail thumped weakly.

Then Alec said, 'She'll do. OK. Now tell me what happened.'

Liza had turned away to the sink, busying herself with the gloves and instruments.

'I'd been to supper with a friend,' the man said. 'Wendy and I were walking home. We're often out after dark. We know all the streets of the Estates like the back of our hand. Or paw. But something happened. We were getting near the pub – I can smell the beer fifty yards off – and there were people shouting and running and someone must have thrown a bottle. I heard it crash just as Wendy moved to protect me. I put my hand down and felt the blood and then suddenly this girl was there. She was marvellous. The blood was spurting out. She put on a tourniquet. I think she saved Wendy's life.'

'Oh shut up, anyone can put on a tourniquet,' Liza said.

'What did you use?' Tom asked.

'My sock.' She giggled and turned round. She had one knee sock and one bare leg under frayed, cut-off blue jeans. 'My last pair.'

'I'll buy you some more.' The blind man smiled, and Liza said, 'Ta.' They seemed to have come to a friendly understanding. 'She carried the dog here,' he told Alec. 'You weren't in, but she had the keys.'

'There's no other vet for miles,' Liza said quickly, 'or I wouldn't have come.'

'Why not?'

'Well – you know.' She swung her red hair forward to hide her face. Then she lifted her head and looked Alec boldly in the eye. 'I took the money.'

'I don't care, Red. Your mother told me why.'

'You don't *care*? I thought you'd put the police on me. I been hiding. I been all over trying to get work. I came back here because I – because – oh hell, I don't know why I came back, except that I thought somehow I could get some money and pay you back. I will too. I been hiding out with some hippies in that empty house the other side of the park. Got a few nights' work over Christmas, washing glasses at the pub. I saw who threw the bottle.'

'They almost killed Wendy,' the blind man said, stroking the dog's head. 'You ought to tell the police.'

'No fear.' Liza laughed. 'Not me.'

When the yellow labrador was bedded down for the night, Alec said he would drive her owner home and then take Liza back to World's End.

'Tom's sleeping here,' he told her. 'He's helping me with a hip joint operation early tomorrow.'

'What's this?' Liza turned to Tom. 'Trying to take over my job?'

'I've been keeping it open for you,' he said, 'you stupid dope.'

'Carrie!'

Carrie thought the whisper was in her dream. But she woke, and Liza was standing by her bed.

'Where's Dusty?'

'Oh, Liza.' Carrie sat up. 'He's dead.'

'Tom didn't tell me.'

'You've seen him? He couldn't, I suppose. He thinks it was his fault.'

'So what? If the old dog's dead, he's dead, that's all.' She turned away.

'Take Dump.' Carrie fished under the blanket. 'He's a good puppy.'

'He yours?'

'He doesn't like me,' Carrie lied. 'You have him.'

'OK.' Liza took the spaniel puppy. She never said thank you, but you knew what she meant.

Carrie could not get to sleep again. She went to the window and looked towards the yard. The snow lay bright under the moon. The stable was silver on one side, black on the other, with sharp corners. Leonora coughed her chronic winter cough, and one of the horses snorted.

John. Carrie knew all the sounds of him, as well as all the smells.

She knelt with her arms on the sill and her head on her arms, staring through the frost patterns on the glass. When John came to the window and she rode him up to the Star, his hoofs rang hollow on the icy sky.

On the Star, it was always spring. The grass was always fresh and green. The horses never grew muddy winter coats and long burr-tangled tails.

Most of them had forgotten what Christmas was, but one American Morgan horse remembered pulling a sleigh to church at midnight, and being given a bag of carrots and a bucket of ale.

Carrie had given John a new halter, which Miss Etty had helped her to make out of different coloured cords braided together. He showed it off, turning his plain bony head this way and that with his eyelashes lowered.

'Cissy,' a carthorse jeered. 'It will be a plastic browband next, no doubt.'

'What's wrong with that?' Priscilla's bay show pony jumped a low rail with as much flourish as if it was a five-barred gate. 'I had a green shiny browband with stars on it. They twinkled.'

'If a horse could throw up,' John said, 'I would.'

'How is – er – what's-her-name?' the show pony asked.

She pretended not to care, but being a horse, and therefore basically good-natured, she did feel bad about Priscilla.

'Grounded,' John said, 'for lack of money.'

'Money, what's that?' The carthorse stared stupidly, his moustached lip hanging.

'It's what you can't get anything on earth without,' Carrie said bitterly. 'If we can't pay for the barn roof to be mended, Priscilla can't ride for the rest of the winter. Money spoils everything. It made Liza run away. She stole some, I think.'

On the Star, you could tell any secret, because the only people who came from earth were dead already and looking for their horses.

'Stealing is wicked,' a black, big-footed police horse said smugly.

'She stole me.' John turned his head in the fancy halter and nudged at Carrie's bare toe. 'Out of a pig van.'

'My dear,' said the show pony, 'spare us the grisly details of your past.'

Twenty

Every morning and every afternoon, Jerome Fielding watched for the Post Office van to bring him a letter about his book. Sometimes it slowed and Dad ran out across the iron-frosted lawn, jumped the snow-filled ditch before the postman opened his door, then turned and slogged dejectedly back with a bill or a circular or a picture postcard from one of his world-wide café acquaintances.

One morning, he could stand it no longer. After breakfast, he yelled up the stairs for Em.

She had been lying on the small floor space of her cupboard room, reading her play. In the last scene, the heroine

111

was tied to the stake for burning because she would not betray her lover. Em wept behind her eyes, as the audiences would weep.

'Want to come to London?'

Em got up at once and collected the papers into the cracked satchel which she now took everywhere, in case someone got at the play. She slung it on her shoulder and jumped down the crooked stairs, with ink on her hands and face, dust on the front of her jeans.

'In a skirt,' Dad said. 'We are going to try and sell ourselves to the Editor of the *Daily Amazer*.'

They waited two hours in the reception room, while impressive, busy people came and went, and the receptionist handled telephone calls that sounded earth-shakingly important.

When they were finally called in, the Editor of the *Daily Amazer* had the manuscript of *Sailor of the Seven Seas* on his wide desk and the photographs of Mother and the boat.

Dad and Em walked nervously over the thick carpet and sat down. The Editor watched them approach, a bald, rosy man who twinkled at Em to show that he was good with children.

'Didn't make a special trip, I hope?'

'Oh no. I have a lot of business to see to.' Dad tried to sound airy, but he fiddled nervously with the gold ring in his ear. He waited for the Editor to say something about his book.

The Editor waited for him.

'So I thought...' Dad uncrossed his legs and crossed them the other way. 'I thought, as long as I was here...' He cleared his throat.

The Editor waited.

'...I'd just drop in to see what you thought of – of the book.'

'To save you a stamp,' Em added politely.

'Good of you.' The Editor smiled. 'I'm sorry.'

Em's heart stopped. Her father had gone white round the edges of his beard.

'Don't you like my book?'

'I *like* it all right. But it's not right for us. Nor are the pictures.'

'What do you mean not right?' Dad stood up.

'We can't use it. I'm sorry.' The Editor held out the manuscript. Em was horrified to see that when her father reached for it, his strong brown hands were shaking.

It was like when someone cuts themself and you see the edges of flesh open and the blood, and you double up in pain because you feel it too. Em could have been sick on the Editor's plushy carpet, as he called her up to take the pile of photographs. On top was the worst one of Mother, her hair wet and stringy, knock-kneed in a faded swimsuit against a sullen grey sky. You could almost hear her teeth chattering.

'Beautiful daughter you have there, Mr Fielding. You should take pictures of *her* in a boat some time. "Child of the Sea." In colour. Those eyes...' He twinkled his own. Em, who usually loved compliments, could only put her head down and stumble for the door.

In the lift, they could not look at each other. In the car, they couldn't talk, not only because of the noise.

Charlie stood on the back seat with his nose to the window, snuffing the draught. Off the main road, taking the short cut through the far corner of the Housing Estates, there was a van blocking their road. Dad opened the window to yell at it to get out of the way.

'Detour.' A man came from behind the van. 'Shooting a film here.'

'What film?' Dad asked belligerently. He was ready to pick a fight with anybody.

'Dog biscuit commercial.'

At the far end of the street, there was a crowd of people, and some dogs on leads.

Dad growled a curse – would he ever smile again? – and crunched into reverse. As he turned to look behind him,

Charlie favoured his nose with a wet mauve tongue.

Dad was already so angry that he hit him in the face. Charlie sneezed. Em burst into tears and climbed into the back seat.

'Go on,' Dad said miserably. 'You turn against me too, like all the rest.' He tortured the gears, wrenched the wheel and skidded forward on the icy road. Charlie lost his balance and fell against his shoulder.

'Get back.' He shrugged him off. 'Useless, stupid dog.'

'He's a genius,' Em mumbled into Charlie's coat.

'Then why doesn't *he* write a book? You work your guts out, and who cares? Dog food commercial, he says. All people care about is some stupid dog.'

Em lifted her face out of Charlie's long hair and said, 'Let me out at the corner. I want to see Alec Harvey.'

'I'll drop you there.'

'I want to walk.'

He jammed on the brakes. The back doors didn't open when you braked like that. Clutching the satchel, Em climbed over the seat to get out. Charlie leaped after her.

'The rats desert the sinking ship,' Dad said bitterly and drove off, polluting Newtown with his broken exhaust pipe.

Em ran back over the dirty town snow to where she had seen the film people. *Which is the producer?* As she ran, she rehearsed what she was going to say. *Here is a play. You can buy it if you want.* The man would look through the pages. *Great stuff. Who wrote it? I did. You?* No. As she ran, Em felt again the pain in the pit of her stomach when her father took the terrible blow in the Editor's office. *My father wrote it. Jerome Fielding.*

She came to the back of a small crowd, and pushed her way through.

'Which is the—'

'Quiet. They're going to shoot.'

'All right, everybody. Quiet please. This will be a take.' A man in dark glasses and a long sheepskin coat with fur round the collar and bottom was shouting through a megaphone in the middle of the street.

114

'Everybody clear now. Georgie, here on the marker with that bloody great box. Everybody else into the houses, or over there out of view. We don't want to see anyone but the dogs. OK, Jack, you're behind the red door with that black and white monstrosity. Nancy, get that dog into the kennel. You know when to give him the signal. You – where's the poodle's trainer? – get him behind the gate and don't let him jump till the brown dog is level. Take him up the street, Wally, behind the wall. We don't see him till the whistle. Mrs What's-it, you're behind the camera. OK everybody, you know what you do. Mrs What's-it blows the whistle. Wally lets the brown dog go, and as he comes down the street you other handlers let your dogs go – through the door flap, over the gate, out of the kennel. Get 'em excited. I want to see them come round this corner yelping like a pack of wolves.'

'While I stand there?' said the man with the outsize box of dog biscuits nervously.

'While you stand there, Georgie. That's why you've got a padded suit. Chuck out the biscuits fast. Maybe they'll go for them.'

Em stood at the front of the crowd with her hand on Charlie's collar.

'Action!'

The whistle blew. The brown dog shot out from behind the wall. The poodle leaped the gate with all four feet together. Charlie tore loose from Em's hand and ran out, shouting. There were seven or eight dogs tearing down the street with Charlie in the lead, scuttering the snow. Running with the horses had made him fast and fit.

Georgie with the padded suit and the dog biscuits stood in the middle of the road with a big actor's grin on his rubbery comedian's face. Charlie reached him first, and as the actor threw a biscuit, he went up on his hind legs with his paws wide apart, dancing and laughing in the snow, catching the biscuits – one, two, three – over his shoulder, high in the air, pouncing down to field a low one right from the jaws of the black and white mongrel.

Two of the dogs started to fight. One crawled under a car. Charlie bounced in front of Georgie with his plumed tail going like a flag, catching the biscuits all round him.

'Cut! That's it – OK everybody, grab your dogs, break it up!' The man in the long Russian coat and dark glasses yelled over the pandemonium of barking dogs. Georgie threw the biscuit box at them and joined the director.

'That shaggy dog stole the scene,' he said.

'Where did he come from?'

Em stepped forward to defend Charlie.

'I let him go. I'm sorry.'

'Don't be. It was great. He's a natural.'

'He was absolutely marvellous.' The actor gave Em his rubbery grin.

'I thought you were very good too,' she said politely.

'You've had your lot though, Georgie,' the Director said. 'From now on, I'm going to use that dog alone. Just the biscuits flying at him from all sides, and we speed it up so he's catching them flick, flick, flick.' He wagged his head until the dark glasses fell into the snow. 'I want him at the studio tomorrow. We'll build the new series round him. What's his name, kid?'

'Charlie.'

Charlie, who had eaten all the biscuit crumbs, and most of the box, looked up.

'Catchem Charlie. I'll make him famous.'

The director bent and kissed Em, which surprised her into the courage to say, 'I brought you a play.' She swung the satchel round to open it. 'It's very good.'

'Don't bother me now, honey. We're going to try another take.'

'Would *you* like a play to act in?' Em asked Georgie.

'No.' The director pulled him away. 'Come on. Another take. Can Charlie do it again?'

Twenty One

Charlie was famous. Catchem Charlie. Children recognized him in the street and shopkeepers were all of a sudden politer.

The day they showed the first commercial, everybody went to Mr Mismo's house to watch it on the huge colour set which took up half the sitting-room.

'Catchem Charlie! He never misses! And your dog will never miss health and fun with Chewitt biscuits!'

Grinning like an alligator, his matted winter coat bathed and brushed, Charlie caught the dog biscuits above, ahead, and all round him.

'He did miss a few,' said Em, who was Head Handler and always went to the studio with him, 'but they cut those bits out.'

At the end of the short commercial, Charlie gave several shouting barks at the camera ('He'll always ask for more!'), and it moved right in on his eager jaws and bright toffee-ball eyes. They thought he would bark back at the screen, but he lay under the tea table and would not look, any more than he would ever look at himself in the mirror.

The advertising agency had paid him some money in advance, and the barn roof was mended within a week.

Carrie and Lester and Michael went to Brookside to tell the Agnews. They rode up the front drive, and Priscilla beat on her turret room window, and they could see her mouth shaping the cry, 'Oliver!'

Oliver was eating an ornamental blue spruce.

'That's poison.' Mr Agnew came to the door in ski trousers and a thick white sweater, looking fit and tanned (he cheated with a sun lamp).

'No, that's yew,' Carrie said.

'I'm harmless.' He liked a good simple joke, and Michael laughed kindly at the ancient pun.

'Will *she* let Bristler ride again?' he asked.

'She doesn't want her to.'

'What about you?' Lester asked.

For all his hearty ways and booming laugh, Mr Agnew was quite easy to talk to, as grown ups go.

'Well – I'd try anything, but Priskie has always been my wife's department,' he said, as if the family were a store.

In the room upstairs, they saw Mrs Agnew shaking her head vigorously. Priscilla's face fell away from the window and they heard her babyish wail.

'She never cries when she's riding,' Michael said.

Mr Agnew put his hands over his ears. 'I can't stand that noise of hers. Sometimes I hear it in the night, but when I go in there, she's not awake. She must cry in her sleep.'

'So you hear it too,' Lester whispered, and Peter moved restlessly as he felt his body tense.

'Hear what?'

They told him about the ghost of Diller's baby, and the tree that wailed when the axe struck it.

'How perfectly marvellous.' His eyes bulged. 'I've never had a haunting before. Why doesn't my wife hear it?'

'There's some people hear ghosts,' Lester said in Miss Etty's tones, 'and some that don't.'

'And I do? I say, how splendid. I'm psychic. She's not.'

'Make her let Bristler ride,' Michael urged quickly.

'Make her?' Discovering that he could hear ghosts had set him up no end. 'If I say she can, she can.'

He ran off lightly on the balls of his feet to tell Priscilla. The wailing stopped. Her face came again to the window, waving and smiling. They waved back. As they turned to go, they could hear the man's and woman's voices raised behind her in argument.

Soon after Priscilla began to ride again in the big barn, she was joined by Mr Mismo's nephew Rickie. He was partly

118

paralysed from polio. He had hobbled on crutches for so long that he could hardly remember when he had played and run with other children.

When Mr Mismo came to ask Alec if he would teach Rickie to ride, he offered his cob, Princess Margaret Rose. 'Quiet as a peastick. You could fire a gun under her nose. I have too.'

'She's too broad.' Alec Harvey knew the mare well. She sometimes went lame, though Mr Mismo said she was 'sound as a dragonfly'. 'And she's a heavy goer.'

'Oh fish, she goes across country like a cloud. Dressage too, in her day.'

When Mr Mismo talked about the fat oatmeal cob, it always sounded as if he were talking about another horse.

Lester offered Peter, but Alec thought he would be too quick and nervous.

'John could do it,' Carrie said. John could do anything.

'Too hot. You been corning him up.' Mr Mismo was not going to let John have it over Princess Margaret Rose.

'I've been giving him Mounted Police training. He'll stand anywhere. If Constable Dunstable ever gets himself moved out of the village, we'll need John for riot control when the Revolution starts.'

'What Revolution?' Mr Mismo tipped back his tweed hat which was shaped like a mould for blancmange, and scratched under his grey forelock.

'Against Mrs Agnew making the Women's Institute do Keep-fit classes in mauve tights,' Lester said. His mother gave talks at the WI on how to stop your daughter doing something that would get her into Mount Pleasant. At the last meeting, Mrs Agnew had told her that if she lost two stone, public speaking would not make her breathless. She had never been back.

John seemed to know what was wanted of him. With Carrie to lead him and Mother walking beside Rickie, he stood still for the exercises, walked on, trotted slow and smooth, carrying the boy as if he were a fragile egg. With two riders, they could have games and competitions.

'It's got to be fun,' Alec said. 'That's what the horses can give them.'

Priscilla and Rickie were having more fun than either of them had known for years.

Before every lesson, they brushed John and Oliver, Rickie propped on his crutches, Priscilla leaning against a wall, but standing more strongly all the time.

Michael gave quizzes on points of the horse.

'What's this lump here at the bottom of his neck?'

Priscilla hung her head. Her memory was terrible, because she had not used it for so long. Rickie gave his slow, gentle smile and shook his head.

'I told you,' Michael said sternly. 'The weathers. What's that there at the top of his bee-hind?'

'Croup!' Priscilla turned round in the saddle and put her hand on top of Oliver's round quarters. When she started exercising on the pony, she could not turn at all.

'All right, now this sort of ankle there is called the fetlock. Rickie, what's the point of the shoulder?'

'To hold his neck on?' Rickie laughed when everyone laughed.

'Show me.'

Rickie leaned to touch the pony's shoulder with his thin, twisted hand. Alec had got the saddler to sew bars across the reins so he could hold them with his two good fingers, and John could neck-rein like a cowpony. They had slow bending races round poles cemented into flower pots.

On the Star one night, John told a group of horses about his new job.

'I won a bending race today.'

'Pooh, that's nothing.' The flighty bay mare who had crushed Priscilla's back tossed her head as if she could feel the rosette under her ear. 'I won at millions of gymkhanas. Full gallop.'

'I won in a walk,' John said.

'So did I.' Creeping Sally bumped him with her blind old head. 'A hundred years ago, I won a trotting match in a fog that stopped all the others, even Phenomena. My rider and I had no use of our eyes anyway.'

'My rider has no use of his legs,' John said. 'He uses mine.'

He and Carrie walked back down through the skies, dropping gently towards sleep. The poem in Carrie's head was the rhythm of his ambling walk:

What if we still ride on, we two.
With life for ever old yet new . . .
. . . And heaven just prove that I and she
Ride, ride together, for ever ride?

When Carrie died, she would ride John for ever on the limitless turf of the Star.

Twenty Two

Charlie got another payment for the Chewitt Dog Biscuit commercials, and they bought two lorry loads of sand and wood shavings for the floor of the barn.

The doctor wanted a spastic child to join the riding class, so a girl from the Pony Club brought her roan New Forest in a trailer twice a week. Helpers volunteered. The group was going to be part of the Riding for the Disabled Association.

'It's mad,' Mrs Agnew still declared, but it was working.

Once, Priscilla walked three steps before she clutched at Oliver's neck.

Her father, coming to fetch her, did not believe it.

'Do it again, Bristler,' Michael ordered. She did it.

'It's fantastic,' Mr Agnew told Alec, 'what you're doing.'

'It's not us,' Alec said. 'It's the pony.'

*

121

Mrs Agnew had kept away, but after Priscilla walked three steps, she finally agreed to come and watch her ride. It was a freak warm day, so they went out to the flat corner at the bottom of the meadow.

Mrs Agnew was very nervous. 'Look out!' she called when Oliver stumbled. Priscilla turned to look at her and lost the rhythm.

'Look at me, Pris,' Alec called. 'Rickie, get that heel down. Susan, come on, you can rise to the trot. Legs, Pris, legs! Push him on. A lazy rider means a lazy horse.'

'She's not lazy,' Mrs Agnew told him when he came over to the fence where she was sitting. 'She can't use her legs.'

'It's what they *can* do that counts,' Alec said. 'Not what they can't. Look at 'em.'

Under a pale winter sun, two girls and a boy trotted round on the grass. Two wheelchairs stood by the gate and a pair of crutches leaned against the fence.

Lined up for exercises, they had to lean back on the quarters. If Michael lay on Oliver's back, he bucked. With Priscilla, he had learned to stand still, though he put back his ears and tossed his head.

'Watch that pony!' Mrs Agnew called to Michael.

He looked round at her as she jumped down from the fence right behind Oliver. Oliver started, and trod on Michael's toe. He yelled. Oliver jumped sideways. Liza grabbed at Priscilla, and managed to knock her foot out of the stirrup as she fell, toppling over the pony's quarters with a thump on to the frosted ground that was as loud as Mrs Agnew's cry.

She lay for a moment half stunned, then as her mother ran up and knelt beside her, she began to wail. Mrs Agnew picked her up and walked towards the gate. Priscilla wailed louder.

'I want Oliver!'

'She's all right.' Alec had checked her. 'Put her back on. It's the only thing after a fall.'

'You must be mad, Mr Harvey. I knew something like this would happen. You stupid child.' She rounded on

Priscilla fell, toppling over the pony's quarters with a thump.

Michael. 'That pony's mean, I knew it.'

Michael led Oliver away from her and tied him to the fence. Carrie would give him hell if she saw that he had tied him by the reins, but he didn't care. He didn't care about anything except that he had ruined the riding for Priscilla.

Her mother had put her in her wheelchair and was standing in a group, arguing with the other grown ups. Priscilla sat hunched miserably, like a trapped sparrow.

Michael pulled his hood low over his frowning eyes and limped up the hill, kicking tufts of grass. He had to get away where no one could see him. He sat down under the lone elm in the middle of the slope. Tomorrow and tomorrow and tomorrow ... he would go on feeling as bad as this for the rest of his life. If he knew how to kill himself, he would.

As he sat under the tree with his nose running in the cold and his hands turning blue and purple, he saw Priscilla drag herself up out of the chair. She lost her balance and toppled against it. It fell sideways as she staggered forward and grabbed the fence. Then she began to pull herself along the fence, half dragging her feet, half hobbling. Carrie with John, the Pony Club girl with the roan pony, the arguing grown ups, all had their backs to her.

When she reached Oliver, she leaned against his neck. He turned his seahorse head and nudged her, nearly making her lose her frail balance. She untied his reins, and managed, leaning against him, to put them back over his neck.

'*Stand!*' Michael whispered, from a hundred yards away. As if he heard, Oliver's head went up, his small furred ears tipped forward. He stood.

Somehow, with the effort of climbing Mount Everest, Priscilla hauled herself up to stand on the middle rail of the fence, swung over her leg, and was in the saddle.

Michael stood up. He saw her feeble legs swing back to squeeze the pony. Oliver moved forward.

'Priskie!' The group turned. Mrs Agnew started forward, but her husband took her hand and held her back.

Suddenly, she relaxed. 'Ride, Priskie!' she called, and began to laugh. 'Go on, my clever – ride!'

Michael began to run down the hill. Priscilla pushed the pony into a trot and rode towards him alone, her dark eyes shining, her mouth stretched wide in a grin of triumph.

The wheelchair lay on its side in the grass. She was free.

If you have enjoyed this Piccolo Book,
you may like to choose your next book from
the titles listed on the following pages.

Monica Dickens

Follyfoot 30p

Here we meet for the first time the people and horses who live
at the farm on the top of the hill. There's always so much to do
at the farm – tending unwanted horses, providing mounts for
film companies, schooling ponies, helping unlucky
holidaymakers and keeping a wary eye on the unscrupulous
owners of the Pinecrest riding stables – life can never be dull for
Callie and her family!

Dora at Follyfoot 30p

More exciting adventures at the Follyfoot farm! This time, the
Captain has to go away, and he leaves everything in the charge
of Dora and Steve, warning them – with an eye on the finances –
'Don't buy any more horses!' But Dora knew she just had to
buy Amigo, the rangy, scarred, cream-coloured horse – and to
pay back the money she borrows, someone from Follyfoot
simply has to win the Moonlight Pony Steeplechase . . .

(Both these stories are based on the highly popular Yorkshire
TV series.)

Enid Blyton

The Island of Adventure 40p
The Castle of Adventure 40p
The Valley of Adventure 40p
The Sea of Adventure   40p

Follow the adventures of Jack, Lucy-Ann, Philip, Dinah,
Bill Smugs and Kiki the parrot through this exciting series,
and watch for:

The Mountain of Adventure
The Ship of Adventure
The Circus of Adventure
The River of Adventure

soon to be published as Piccolo titles.

Maria Gripe

Josephine 25p
Hugo 25p
Hugo and Josephine 25p

This Swedish trilogy is justly acclaimed for its humorous but
sensitive account of two young lives: Josephine, the youngest
daughter of a country parson, and Hugo, the only son of a
charcoal maker.

Lavinia Derwent

Sula 25p
Return to Sula 25p

Magnus really prefers animals to people. And on Sula, the
remote island where he lives, he has many friends, his favourite
being 'Old Whiskers' the seal, with whom he spends most of his
time.

Honor Arundel

The High House 20p
Emma's Island 20p
Emma in Love 25p

This humorous and realistic trilogy describes Emma's life from
the time she is orphaned at thirteen and goes to live with her
absent-minded aunt in Edinburgh to the time she is sixteen and
sets up as housekeeper to her student brother.

These and other Piccolo books are obtainable from all booksellers
and newsagents. If you have any difficulty please send
purchase price plus 7p postage to

PO Box 11 Falmouth Cornwall